THE HOLMBURY COUNTY SEAT WAR

Who really was involved in the brutal massacre of a small village at the start of the American Civil War, and what became of them? In this bitter tale, the truth doesn't finally emerge until 1887, when good men turned bad fight ruthlessly to ensure that their town is elected as the Holmbury county seat.

K. S. STANLEY

THE HOLMBURY COUNTY SEAT WAR

Complete and Unabridged

LINFORD
Leicester

First published in Great Britain in 2017 by
Robert Hale
an imprint of The Crowood Press
Wiltshire

First Linford Edition
published 2020
by arrangement with
The Crowood Press
Wiltshire

A catalogue record for this book is available
from the British Library.

ISBN 978–1–4448–4490–0

Published by
Ulverscroft Limited
Anstey, Leicestershire

Set by Words & Graphics Ltd.
Anstey, Leicestershire
Printed and bound in Great Britain by
T. J. International Ltd., Padstow, Cornwall

This book is printed on acid-free paper

Prologue

The *New York Times* reporter manoeuvred his way through the throng of chattering people. He felt proud that his editor had sent him to cover a special joint meeting of the Gentlemen's and Ladies' sections of the Grand Army of the Republic, the fraternal organization for Civil War veterans. As he made his way towards the bar, he soaked up the atmosphere: the laughter of people enjoying themselves, the clink of glasses raised in celebration, the smell of cigar smoke. The cub reporter spotted his target interviewee, Floyd Greenburn, seated at the end of the long bar, pouring his first glass of the evening from a bottle of whiskey while talking with his wife. Having made his way over to them, the *New York Times* man introduced himself to Floyd and

Floyd's delightful wife, Sarah. The men shook hands, and as they sat down to talk, Sarah excused herself. Floyd picked up his glass and listened intently as the reporter asked his first question. The old man took a sip of his whiskey while he marshalled his thoughts. He then put the glass back on the bar and began to speak.

'Well, I remember bein' mighty shocked at the time. I was only seventeen in 1861 an' consequently too young to fight in the Civil War, but when I heard the news I felt my world had been smashed apart, yer know? That feelin' when yer body goes numb, an' those fight or flight chemicals are tryin' to kick in, but yer stay rooted to the spot, paralysed by shock.'

'Was that when yer first heard the news about your cousin bein' involved in the atrocity?' the cub reporter asked, hanging on to Greenburn's every word.

'Yep, that's right. Milt was three years older than me an' I loved him to bits. Known 'im since I was a toddler, the elder brother I never had, so I knew what I was hearin' wasn't right. Milt didn't have a bad bone in his body. Never did have, never could have.'

'But as second in command, your cousin was hung for leading the massacre, wasn't he, as of course were the men under him?'

'Yep, they sure were. I was actually there, as were many of the population in the barracks town where those soldiers were stationed. Ten men died that day on those gallows. All hung at the same time. The hangman walked along the line of 'em releasin' one trap door after another, barely breakin' stride. But, kid, an' here's the thing — that wasn't justice. Retributive justice maybe, but not true honourable justice.'

'But didn't your cousin's unit kill two dozen men, women and children? There has to be rules about war doesn't there, and how far you can go?' the reporter asked, sensing he might be on to a very good story.

'Listen, kid,' Greenburn spat angrily. 'You must have read the archives, the Union ones at least. The Confederates were getting hammered in that dangerous area on the border, between the Unionists and the secessionist states, yet they had superior resources. It was as if the Unionists had inside information about Confederate troop positions. An' that border was jest a political one. It didn't mean if you stood a hundred yards to the north of it, yer didn't support slavery, or if yer lived a hundred yards to the south of it, yer didn't wanna be part of the Union. Things rarely work that neatly. So the Confederates became suspicious of disloyalty in people they had considered their supporters. Confederate spies confirmed that not only was this the case, but the women and children were as much involved in trading information for food, as the menfolk. So, my cousin's unit was sent into the village to arrest the ringleaders, and that's when things started to fall apart.'

'How do you know all this?' the reporter asked. 'You are putting forward detail that isn't in the public archives.'

'Because my cousin told me,' Greenburn replied, 'an' I know he wouldn't have lied to me. If he'd deserved to be hung, he would have told me. Floyd, he'd have said, I played with fire an' I got burnt, so I deserve to die. My cousin was a courageous, honourable man.'

'How come you got to speak with him after the massacre?' The reporter looked puzzled. 'I understood the men arrested were not allowed visitors and the trial was a military one behind closed doors.'

'An' that was because it was a cover-up,' Floyd pointed out. 'The Confederate army had screwed it big time. The public were livid an' wanted scalps, while the army needed to protect those higher up who should have known better. So, they closed ranks and sacrificed those near the bottom. It's their way of dealin' with that type of situation. An' it often happens, yer know. Because where there's war, then atrocities are never far away. Fightin' can sometimes do that to a man. Distort his values and his sense of morality. Even a good man.' The reporter looked shocked at the accusations.

'Let me explain,' Greenburn continued. 'I spoke to my cousin Milt briefly, after his arrest while he was on his way to prison. He was in the meat wagon with the others. It was a metal cage on wheels drawn by two horses. I was standing a little way up the street, jest north of the barracks, when I saw the dust cloud in the distance. The horses were in no hurry and neither was their driver. It was as though they wanted to go slow to give the jeerin' crowds on the boardwalks a chance to ogle an' spit at the trapped prisoners inside. The crowds tried to get close to the cage as it rumbled down the street an' touch the men inside. Scuffles began to break out. Soldiers tried to hold the public back, but they were only part successful cos there wasn't enough of 'em, most of the soldiers bein' outta town an' fightin' at the front. The few that remained tried firin' their rifles in the air but it had little impact. An' there was no way they were gonna bring more shame to the town an' actually fire at the people, leastways that's what I thought.

'So, as the prison wagon came near me, I rushed out with some others an' forced my way to the front. I was able to grab hold of the metal wagon bars with both hands. I saw my cousin sittin' on the floor at the back. He didn't look in good shape. I called out to him. Although he looked pleased to see me I could tell he was in pain.

''Cousin Floyd,' he shouted out. 'I've been shot in the arm and the leg.' I was able to see where he'd been crudely patched up. Blood was still soakin' through the bandages. 'I ain't done nothin' wrong, Floyd,' my cousin continued, wincin' with the pain from his wounds. 'I tried to stop it. It was the unit commander who started it. He ordered the massacre and opened the firin'. It was like he was so angry or frightened or a mixture of both, that he started raging like an animal. The fact that those villagers did not bear arms was irrelevant. Their non-violent actions and disloyalty had caused good men to die, and that maddened him to the point of wantin' retributive justice. I threw down my guns an' refused to take part, an' as actin' deputy commander, urged the others to do the same. But the captain shot me in the arm an' the leg. Said he'd deal with me later once everyone in the village had been killed. The other men killed with him out of fear. Eventually another part of the company turned up, but it was too late. They found one little girl afterwards, still alive. Her mother had hidden her in a cellar so she didn't see nothin'. The commander told 'em that I had ordered the massacre and that he had tried to stop me by shootin' me — but by then the men's bloodlust was all fired up.''

'Who was the commander, cousin?' I asked.

''I can't say, here,' Milt replied. 'Too dangerous, makin' accusations against an officer,' he said, reducing his voice to a whisper. 'Here!' He reached into his pocket and took out a small screwed up piece of paper. 'His name's on there.'

'Then a voice shouted from behind me, 'Gimme that!' Clenchin' my fist, I raised my left arm upwards and drove my elbow sharply backwards into the man's stomach. As I heard him gasp for air I kicked the heel of my boot hard against his shin. He grunted in pain. He was a soldier.

''Get 'im!' shouted the soldier's colleague as he fired his rifle in the air. I ran across the street, bolted down an alleyway and headed for the scrubland that marked the town limits, as fast as I could. The soldier was chasin' after me but I was young, quick, an' not carryin' any equipment, unlike my pursuer. I bounded through the scrub and soon made the edge of the woods. I felt good, knowin' that I could outrun the man behind me, an' now that I was in amongst the trees, he would find it difficult to fire his rifle. But then, disaster happened. It must have been uneven ground or possibly a rabbit hole or somethin' but I sprained my ankle and fell to the ground. Out of breath, I crawled behind a big bush. I knew that soldier would soon be gainin' on me.

'I took out the piece of paper Milt gave me and unravelled it to reveal the name of the man who had ordered the village massacre: Captain Ransom Travis. I'd never heard of 'im before, but a Confederate captain doin' somethin' like that? Wow! I tore the paper into small pieces and threw them under the bush. I froze as I heard the soldier approachin' an' took out the Army Colt from my trouser belt. I could start to make out the grey colour of his uniform through the leaves of the bush, as they fluttered in the breeze. An' then he saw me.

'I looked him in the eye as best as I could. Holding my pistol with both hands I pulled back the hammer ready to fire. I felt myself shakin'. I'd shot a few wild rabbits before, an' a prairie dog once, but never a human bein'. I felt the beads of sweat rollin' down my face an' droppin' off the end of my chin. I stared hard at the soldier. He was a good few years older than me — an ugly man, it has to be said. We were that close that I could see all the details of his face; the stubble on his chin, the scar on his cheek, the missin' teeth, an' the bloodshot eyes. He'd obviously been drinkin', but many soldiers did that to help anaesthetize their emotions and counter boredom. He could tell that I was a first timer, an' with a wicked grin on his face, attached the bayonet to his rifle.

'Now, that is a horrible way to die, as slow an' painful as the attacker wants to make it. An' this soldier didn't look like the merciful type. He moved back several yards to take a run at me. A feeling of fear coursed through my body. I had to shoot now or I was goin' to die. But I couldn't! My whole body was shakin'! I jest couldn't kill another human bein'! The soldier started his run. I closed my eyes and pulled the trigger. There was a thump as the man fell to the ground, an' then silence. I opened my eyes — the man was dead. I rolled over and threw up under the bush.'

'That's fascinating, Mister Greenburn, so was that what prompted you to enlist?'

'Sure was. The massacre, the wrongful hangin' of my cousin, the cover-up to protect the Captain. So as soon as I was eighteen, I enlisted in the Union army to avenge my cousin's death by the Confederates. They taught me how to be a professional fighter — to only kill when necessary, how to use weapons responsibly and in a disciplined way. You know, if you go to war, you only do so because eventually you think you can win it, which means like it or not, you're in the business of killin' people. So you must do that as efficiently and painlessly as you can, in order to get the peace back, as quick as possible. If you indulge in atrocities, not only will you not do that, but you will have sold your soul to the devil, and no riches on earth will buy your soul back for you.

'Unfortunately, if not managed right, not only can war make a good man turn bad, but ultimately it can trigger any latent tendencies that can turn a man mad. The costs for humanity don't bear thinkin' about.'

'So, briefly, what advice, based on your experience of the Civil War, would you give our young soldiers who set sail tomorrow?'

'Well, I would say watch each other's backs, apply your training diligently, and remember that on behalf of a democratic and free country, you have been asked to fight a just war against the spread of tyranny.'

'Oh, and one last question please,'

said the reporter, seeing Sarah making her way back towards them. Floyd nodded. 'Tell me,' the reporter said, 'did you ever find out what became of Captain Ransom Travis?'

'Yeah. Matter of fact I did,' said Floyd. 'But that's a whole different story — and a different war, too — the Holmbury County Seat War that was, back in '87.'

★   ★   ★

An interview in the summer of 1917 between the New York Times and Floyd Greenburn, a Civil War veteran, on the eve of US troops setting sail across the Atlantic for Europe, to fight in World War I.

1

Adison Marson was oblivious to the coldness of that particular summer night in 1887. Although the small oil lamp on his desk lit up the room so that he could work, it threw out precious little warmth. A lesser man, a younger man even, may have shivered — but not Adison. He was fired up by the warmth of his mission: to find out what really happened in Honer County over twenty-five years ago.

Post the atrocity, when a whole village was razed to the ground, the military decided to pull down the local Confederate army barracks. It was as if the only way they could cope with their shame was to expunge every physical trace of their presence: a kind of out of sight, out of mind mentality. Some pointed out that such behaviour was almost a public admission of guilt.

A compromise of sorts was reached, whereby it was agreed that a small museum should be built, in recognition of the fact that a civil war had actually taken place. However, another part of the compromise was that the museum should not be located in Honer County, but further north, in Holmbury County, and its contents and displays heavily censored by the county seat town of Russen. This was not seen by those involved as in any way fraudulent. After all, history is just a historian's interpretation, and over time subject to reinterpretation. The important thing was being able to move on with some sense of honour and justice.

The museum's seventy-five-years-old curious curator, Adison Marson, did not see things quite the same as the authorities, however. Instinctively he felt that 'under the table' there were still some truths floating around, and that a more accurate interpretation could be made, if these were allowed to surface and could be placed out in the open for all to see. For example, Captain Travis was given a free pardon by the military court. Travis's defence was that he had tried to stop the brutal killings, not start them. Now, if that were so, then why hadn't the army made some attempt to honour such bravery? Instead, Travis had seemingly just vanished off the face of the earth. How come? Such questions excited and energized Adison. And as he had started to make some headway with his enquiries, it had begun to become a mission for him — a purpose for living through what otherwise might have been an empty old age.

There was more. His research had thrown up some information about the other part of the company, who, the court had accepted, had arrived on the scene some fifteen minutes after the atrocity finished. The unit leader, Captain Emmett Aldstone, verified Travis's account of events to the court, claiming that he had seen the slaughter from afar whilst approaching the site

17

where the carnage took place. But just like Ransom Travis, Emmett Aldstone had also surprisingly vanished. As regards the four men under Aldstone's command and with him at the time, verified reports stated that following the atrocity, two had continued to serve in the Civil War but had died in action. Unconfirmed reports, however, claimed that the other two had been murdered, shot through the forehead, although no one had been convicted of the crime. But the real big find for Adison was that he had managed to uncover some new evidence suggesting there was a tombstone bearing the name of Captain Ransom Travis, in a graveyard down south.

A systematic person, Adison had duly sent this information to the county records clerk at Russen, along with his weekly report of the museum's income, expenditure and visitor numbers. With the recent election of a new, enterprising and wealthy state governor, William Peters, Adison felt a change in the air and had recently written to Peters, requesting state funding to visit the grave. He still hadn't received a response, but assumed that the new governor was, no doubt, extremely busy and would get to his request in the fullness of time. Pre-empting this, tonight's particular reason for Adison's preoccupation was the planning of his trip to the grave, in order to confirm Travis's death and thereby fill in another missing piece of the jigsaw puzzle.

With all this going on in his mind, the cold of that summer night was not the only thing that Adison Marson was oblivious to. He was also oblivious to the sound of horses' hoofs in the distance. It started as a low drumming sound, which steadily increased in volume, and suggested the approach of more than one rider. In fact, his conscious mind only became aware of this possibility when the droning sound it had originally dismissed as background noise, stopped. He listened to the silence, and hearing nothing unto-ward, continued with his work.

It was the sudden assault on all of his senses which made Adison Marson realize that his life was potentially in great danger. Being an old man, his hearing was weak but it was his strong sense of smell that first alerted him to the fact that there was a wood fire very nearby. As he got up and moved towards his room door, he could taste the soot from the woodsmoke — and when he opened the room door to look down the stairs, he was momentarily knocked back by the blast of heat from the museum area below. He could see the flames licking up the stairs like a fire-breathing dragon, slowly crawling its way towards him and devouring everything in its path. He could hear the spit and crackle of its salivation as timbers crashed down in its wake.

Adison realized that he had to get down to the mezzanine before the fire reached there, from below. There was a window on the small mezzanine, which he should just about be able to squeeze through; it overlooked the water tank outside, and with the aid of the ladder on the side of the tank he would be able to lower himself to the ground. In his race to get down the stairs, he stumbled and fell, losing vital seconds. He picked himself up and put his head and one leg through the window opening. He twisted and turned within its frame, trying to squeeze the rest of his body through the gap, the flames licking at his trailing ankle. Finally, with the lower half of his left trouser leg now on fire, he pulled himself clear of the window and dived into the tank of cold water to quench the flames.

★   ★   ★

The rope ferryman said good night to the lone rider as he disembarked on the west bank of the River Russen, the only customer on that final journey of the day. The rider raised his hand to acknowledge the civility, noticing, as he did so, an orange glow in the night sky a few miles away, to his left. So instead of turning north and riding to Denton, as would have been his normal practice, he decided to ride south and take a look.

As the rider approached the smouldering ruin he wondered if the old man who lived there and looked after the place was still alive. He rode slowly around the perimeter of what had been the Civil War museum. Parts of the walls were still standing, but basically the place had been gutted by fire. He rode over to the water tank, the only part of the building still completely intact, thanks to its protective metal skin. As he looked inside, he saw the body of Adison Marson floating face up in the water, with a bullet through his forehead.

2

Situated at the southern end of the gorge and on the east bank of the River Russen, the Holmbury county seat town of Russen had, in more recent times, taken on the Saturday night airs and graces found in some eastern seaboard towns. For example, the ladies dressed in their finery could be found perambulating along Main Street on the arms of their beaux, prior to dining at one of the hotels or visiting one of the town's two theatres.

The days of the big cattle drives had already ended for Russen, thanks largely to the invention of barbed wire, which enabled people to enclose their land, and as a result the town's two-and-a-half thousand citizens had grown used to their weekends being sedate and relaxed affairs. Gone were the cribs and the low-end whore houses, the rowdy saloons and the fighting and shooting beloved by the cattle drovers as they hit town, hell bent on a good time.

This gentrification attracted respectable folk from other parts of the county, such as the small market garden town of Faux-Port, slightly north of Russen but on the west bank of the river, and the forestry town of Denton, almost as small, north of Faux-Port. Visitors from these places would either cross the river via the rope ferry which connected the county seat town with the west bank, or travel downstream by steamboat to Russen harbour. After disembarking they were free to enjoy the sophisticated entertainment that a Saturday night had to offer, with many staying overnight.

★　★　★

There were, however, small signs that the rowdy behaviours of the old boom town were starting to reoccur, which gave the mayor, Ezra Danneville, more sleepless nights than many would have imagined. His attempts to explain his concerns and discuss possible strategies with his councillors had met with little success, and Ezra therefore welcomed the opportunity presented by a visit from the newly elected state governor and railroad tycoon, William Peters.

'So, tell me precisely what bothers you, Ezra, about the future of Russen,' the state governor demanded. 'I need to understand the issues of the day, and how big or small people perceive them to be.'

'Well, as you know, the town became rich during the boom years of the cattle drives,' Ezra explained. 'We are fortunate to still be living off the back of that because people were prudent with their new gotten wealth, but eventually that well will run dry because at the moment there is nothing to top it up with. We hold the county seat, and that helps with the revenue from tax collection and county court fees, but in spite of being the county seat, we don't have a railroad.'

'And what about Grainger's Cove, north of Russen? That's fast becoming a boom mining town, and it's actually bigger in terms of population than Russen, isn't it?' Peters asked. The state governor had done his homework.

'It's about three thousand people,' Ezra confirmed, 'but as we both know, mining towns come and go fast. Gold found yesterday leads to reports today that there are vast untapped quantities underground, only to find that tomorrow, in reality, there is virtually nothing. A gamble. But, and here's the thing, those miners — and there is a big number of them coming not only from the south, but the east and west as well — all pass through Russen. I am seeking investment to build a 'hell-on-wheels town' just north of here, so that they pass through Russen very quickly, drawn by the magnet of what such a tent town might offer them, en route to their ultimate destination of the Cove.

What d'you think? Can you help me with this one?'

'That's sounds a sensible short-term tactical solution,' the governor said, 'but what about the strategic issue that underlies it?'

'Do you mean if the Cove is sustainable in the long term as a successful mining town?' Ezra asked.

'Yes,' the governor answered. 'As you are no doubt aware — and this is possibly the more covert motivation behind your questions — there is already pressure from the Cove to have a referendum on which town should hold the county seat.' Ezra recognized that this man was nobody's fool, but intelligent, sharp and direct to the point. It tied in with his own view that logic and principles should always outweigh sentiment.

'If that means there has to be a referendum, then so be it,' Ezra said with conviction. 'The people of Russen won't stand in the way. Democracy must prevail, because it matters.'

'My view entirely,' Governor Peters agreed. 'In my position, not only do I want to promote such a call for a referendum, but I need to be seen to be incentivizing it. Therefore I am proposing to build a railroad from the winning town to other parts of the growing state network.'

'Gee!' said Ezra quite taken aback by the audacity of the governor's plans. 'But what if the Cove wins and in the long term its prosperity proves to be of a far shorter duration?'

'Hm,' William murmured with a knowing smile on his face. 'It's only our first meeting, Ezra, but I like you, and I can see that you are an astute thinker and a man of principle. So — and this is in the strictest confidence — what I just told you was the state governor talking. If we were to allow the railroad man to speak, he would say that if you were to look at the geography of Holmbury County and how it interacts with the economic geography of the state, then there is only one natural transport hub, and that is Russen. It is on the Holmbury Flats with easy access to the east side of the river, it also oversees the most natural east-west crossing point, and on a south-north axis is able to skirt the Holmbury Heights going north.'

'And if any of the other towns are successful in a democratic vote?' Ezra asked.

'Then their spur would get built first, in the spirit of winning the prize. In reality of course, it wouldn't be of much benefit until the hub is built and they are connected to it,' William pointed out, looking very confidently into Ezra's eyes. 'Does that help with your deliberations, Ezra?'

'Yes, thank you, Governor. It certainly does.'

'Good,' William continued, 'because in your role as the mayor of the county seat, there is something I need to ask of you.' He paused momentarily, for Ezra to give a nod of acceptance. 'I have been invited to Washington to a state governors' meeting, next week. It is being hosted by President Grover Cleveland so, as the new kid in town, I don't want anything going disastrously wrong here during the time I'm away. I should be back sometime Wednesday, so I am putting you in charge of ensuring my wishes are carried out. Is that OK with you, Ezra?'

'Yes indeed, Governor,' Ezra replied humbly. He knew he needed to keep on the right side of this man, because it sounded as if, one way or another, his town was going to end up at the centre of a railroad linking it to the rest of the state!

★ ★ ★

On the night of the Saturday that the state governor had left for Washington, Main Street and its adjoining roads could be described as bustling — that is, high spirited but still civilized. Inevitably there was the occasional display of rowdy behaviour, virtually always involving small groups of excited prospectors, who were taking a well-earned 'traveller's rest' before pushing on to the Cove the next morning. The local gentry's response was equally predictable: they looked down their noses and crossed to the other side of the street. Which was why no one, apart from the perpetrators, realized at the time that the rowdy incident that took place mid-evening behind the town hall, involving drunken singing and the firing of a gun, had more sinister undertones.

Indeed, the firing of the gun in question was not the act of drunken revelry that passers-by thought it was, but a sober, premeditated act, designed to breach the lock on the back entrance to the town hall. With that part of their mission discreetly accomplished, the supposed revellers faded away quietly into the night, only to return in the small hours of Sunday morning. With the streets empty, the town quiet and the inhabitants sleeping soundly, their bellies full from the previous night's indulgence, the final part of the mission could be executed with equal efficiency and stealth.

Four masked men carrying a civil war hospital stretcher quietly entered the town hall offices. They loaded a wooden chest containing the county seat records on to the stretcher, which they hoisted on to their shoulders like pall bearers carrying a coffin, and quietly made their way down to the edge of the river. They placed the chest carefully in the bottom of their rowing boat, climbed aboard and silently slipped away from the shore. Possession of the contents of the wooden chest was seen by many as being nine-tenths of the law, thereby giving its new owners claim to the county seat of Holmbury County and all of the privileges that went with that. Winning the county seat was seen as the driver of a town's future prosperity. The status of being the administrative centre and seat of government for the county could rapidly attract businesses and settlers, pushing up land prices for the town's founding fathers and investors. It also helped attract the big prize of the railroad coming to town.

⋆ ⋆ ⋆

Ezra Danneville found it hard to conceal his anger when the records clerk informed him of the break-in on his arrival at the office on Monday morning.

'What!' he screamed. 'They shot the lock off and have taken the county records? How will we be able to collect and account for the right amount of tax?' Ezra asked, starting to panic. 'The county's court and administrative systems will grind to a halt! This is sabotage! This has been planned to coincide with the governor's visit to Washington!' He felt himself break into a cold sweat as he realized that it was down to him to deal with this. He couldn't risk

33

sending a wire to Governor Peters in Washington: he definitely didn't want to show this man, who could be a potential benefactor, that he wasn't up to the job. 'Summon the councillors straightaway,' he ordered the clerk. 'We need to hold an extraordinary meeting, immediately.'

★   ★   ★

'I think we have to contact the governor, regardless of the impression he might be trying to create with President Cleveland. He needs to call in the National Guard,' said the treasurer. 'This is no mere criminal act: it is an act of war!'

'I agree, Shelby, I agree,' said the Head of Commerce. 'This is an insult to the people of Russen. The governor, nor indeed the president, will thank us for procrastinating and allowing things to fester.'

'Gentlemen, gentlemen,' Ezra interrupted. He knew he needed to quell the emotion and persuade them to look at rational alternatives. 'We don't even know who's taken the records, so how would the National Guard know where to start looking for them?'

'Well, they can only be in one of three possible places,' Shelby pointed out. 'First of all there's Denton, but Floyd Greenburn and the folks up there ain't interested in being the county seat. They're, what would you say, industrialists, not administrators. Forestry and selling timber is all they are interested in. The people of Faux-Port are even less interested in being the county seat. Market gardeners to a man. We buy their produce and in return do the civil administration for them, as we do for the rest of the county, and I know for a fact that that's the way they like it.

'And that leaves the Cove. Grainger's Cove. I'm surprised that Marlin didn't rename it Bart town after himself. Nothing moves in that place without him taking a cut, whether it's miners, their equipment, food, drink, women or

35

gold. I reckon he's organized the stealing of our records to ensure the governor holds a referendum.'

'And with the way that place is expanding, they could beat us easily in an election, if they mobilized their electorate,' the Head of Commerce chipped in.

'OK, OK, gentlemen, here's what I propose,' Ezra interjected, seeking to close down any more negative talk. The councillors fell silent. They all knew that Marlin Bart had a reputation for being a megalomaniac, and was odds-on favourite to have stolen the records, but they also knew that proving it wouldn't be easy. They welcomed any constructive proposal.

'Thank you, gentlemen,' Ezra said in acknowledgement. 'Floyd Greenburn is one of the best deputy state marshals, if not the best. He is an honourable man and, equally important, will not take crap from anyone. I suggest that we ask him to do some detective work, and see what he can come up with. At the same time I will visit Grainger's Cove and talk with Marlin Bart. I will tell him that we are offering a forty-eight-hour amnesty to whoever has stolen the records, to hand them back, otherwise the governor will be asked to call in the National Guard. That way, we cover all our bets. So, quick show of hands. All in favour?' Ezra looked around the room. 'Good,' he said, 'motion carried.'

3

Floyd's initial enquiries, in the area around Russen town hall, drew a series of blanks. Nobody had heard or seen anything — they were all in bed asleep. Having spent time in the army, Floyd was pretty good at spotting a liar, and was comfortable that everyone had been telling the truth. He realized that the lack of witnesses was all to the credit of those smart adversaries who had planned and carried out the robbery. So he decided to abandon this line of enquiry, go back to Denton and pick up his two sidekicks, Russ Burrell and Chancy Ford, before taking a boat to the Cove and recommencing investigations from there. But as he turned to go, Floyd felt someone tugging at this sleeve.

'Hey, mister!' It was a little old lady. 'Heard you was asking folk if they heard or saw anything untoward on the night of the robbery?'

'That's right,' Floyd said. 'An' who might you be?'

'I'm Maddie Morgan, people roun' here call me mad Maddie, cos I tell it as I see it, an' that often ain't the same way that other folk do!'

'So, what can I do for you, Maddie?'

'No, it's what I can do for you, mister. You see, that robbery you're enquiring about. Well, I heard a noise in the middle of the night. Woke me up it did.'

'So what did you do then, Maddie?' Floyd asked.

'Ah, I knew you'd be interested in what I had to say, mister. Others said you wouldn't, but I jest knew it. Well, I looked out my window. I didn't see no robbers or anything, but I did see a light on down the street in Miss Tamswaite's residence. Upstairs it was. I thought maybe she might have seen somethin' if she was up an' about.'

'And did she?'

'I dunno, mister. I ain't asked her. That's your job.'

'Thank you, Maddie,' Floyd said. 'You've been most helpful. And where will I find Miss Tamswaite's place?'

'It's the temperance shop. If you still enjoy a drink, mister, you ain't likely to know where the temperance place is. Am I right?' Floyd nodded and smiled. 'Jest follow my finger,' Maddie continued, pointing down the street. 'It's jest over there with the white picket fence.'

★　★　★

Floyd read the notice that was painted neatly on the noticeboard by the gate in the picket fence:

The Holmbury County
Temperance Society

Allow us to put you on our
three-step path to Health,
Happiness and Fulfilment.

1. Abstain from excess intake and addiction to alcohol
2. Seek moderation
3. Strive for total abstinence

Meetings: Every Tuesday at 8pm
Exec Director: Miss S. Tamswaite
Exec Trustee: W. Peters

Floyd knocked on the door anticipating that it would be opened by a late middle-aged, intelligent but self-righteous, uncompromising spinster. He was pleasantly taken aback when the door was answered by an unassuming, attractive and demure-looking woman in her early thirties.

'Howdy, ma'am,' he said doffing his hat. 'My name is Floyd Greenburn, and in my role as a part-time deputy state marshal, I have been asked to investigate the illegal removal of the county seat records from the town hall at the weekend.'

'Hello, Mr Greenburn. I am Sarah Tamswaite,' the woman said, offering her delicate hand. 'Pleased to meet you. Do come in.' As he brushed past her, he caught a waft of her perfume. 'I'm afraid the downstairs offices are being redecorated as we speak. I suggest we go upstairs to my residence. This sounds like a matter of integrity and therefore we should seek privacy.'

She smiled gently, looking him directly in the eye, but sensing his slight unease at such directness, turned her head away a little. It was as well. Floyd felt attracted to her as if there were an affinity of sorts between them. Sarah was equally aware of this, but both being afraid of misreading the signals, they let the brief moment pass unspoken, and resumed their respective social roles. Part of hers was obviously that of being a good hostess, and after seeing him comfortably seated in her parlour, she retired to the kitchen to make a pot of coffee.

While she was gone, he looked quickly around the room. So this is how a temperance person lives, he thought to himself. Neat and tidy, but with distinct feminine touches such as the small flower arrangements and displays of trinkets. Without leaving his chair he could see into a cupboard whose door was slightly ajar, and thought he noticed items of men's clothing. On the windowsill opposite, by the kitchen door, he noticed the small squashed stub of a cigar in an ashtray.

Sarah returned and placed a coffee pot and a plate of biscuits on the table. 'I'll just get the cups,' she said, and returned to the kitchen, discreetly removing the ash tray from the windowsill on the way. When she came back she passed him a cup, deliberately holding on to the other one for herself, and indicated to him to help himself to the coffee and biscuits.

'Thanks, Sarah,' Floyd said. 'Sorry — is it OK for me to call you Sarah?'

'Of course,' she replied. She got up and pushed the ajar cupboard door closed. 'How can I help you?'

'I'm trying to find out if anybody saw

anything untoward happen on the night of the robbery. I was told that your light was on in the small hours when the robbery happened, and wondered if you saw anything?'

Sarah blushed. 'No, I'm afraid not,' she said. 'I live alone, and my pleasure comes from reading. I expect my light was on because I was in bed reading, as it helps me go to sleep. Sometimes, when I start to nod off, I prefer to leave the light on rather than wake myself up again by crossing the room and turning it out.'

'I understand. Done similar myself on a number of occasions,' Floyd said, making her feel at ease. 'Oh well, it would have been wrong not to have asked. I'd better go. Thanks for the refreshment.'

'You're welcome,' she said, getting up to hold the door open for him. As he brushed past her skirts and walked through the narrow doorway, he felt the warmth of her breath on his face. He noticed she smelt slightly different.

* ★ *

Floyd walked away from Sarah's house, feeling very intrigued by the two sides of this woman. On the one hand he found her very attractive, a lady with social graces but no false airs, a gentle person. Certainly not a person who could be described as insincere, let alone a liar. So on the other hand, why did she try to deceive? Why had she made a point of saying that she lived alone when there was men's clothing in her cupboard, and a cigar in the ashtray? There could be a very reasonable explanation for these things, of course, but why did she blush when challenged about the light being on? That's often the behaviour of someone who feels forced to lie, but doesn't want to because they are not very good at it. Then there was the different smell about her as he left: the distinctive smell of gin. Maybe she didn't offer him a choice of coffee cup because the one she kept hold of already had a good measure of gin in it before she poured in the coffee. Unusual behaviour for a temperance advocate!

4

Ezra Danneville instinctively turned up his nose as he walked along the main street of Grainger's Cove, on his way to meet Marlin Bart. He couldn't help it. Unlike the eastern seaboard where he had been raised, this place was full of uncivilized roughnecks and a hotbed of sin, greed and disorder. The environment of the Cove, with its muddy streets full of puddles of stagnant rainwater, its humid atmosphere and its large tent city which promoted close, even intimate human contact in its saloons, dance halls and cribs, also had the potential to rapidly spread disease amongst its inhabitants.

At the end of Main Street, Ezra came to one of its few wooden buildings, the aptly named, at least by comparison with some of the other structures, 'Grand Hotel'. This was a three-storey building, with a saloon, gambling facilities and dance hall on the ground floor, a bordello on the first floor, and the proprietor's 'penthouse' on the top floor. Ezra was taken to the top floor by a swarthy-looking man, whose vocabulary consisted more of grunts than words. The Grand's resident owner, Marlin Bart, was there to meet them.

'Howdy, Ezra,' said Marlin through his teeth. 'Come on in.' The characteristic sneer on his face momentarily changed to a crooked smile.

'Good day, Marlin,' Ezra responded, already feeling a sense of irritation at having to be a guest in the devil's den. But he was a man of breeding and manners and wouldn't let his distaste show.

'So, what can I help you with?' asked Marlin, as he poured them both a glass of whiskey.

'It's about the stealing of our county seat records,' Ezra explained. 'The town council of Russen have agreed that we should offer an amnesty to whoever has

48

taken the records, provided that they are returned, intact, within the next forty-eight hours.'

'And that begs the question, what if they're not, don't it?' Marlin replied.

'Yes, and if they are not, I will contact the state governor in Washington to call in the National Guard.'

'So, why are you telling me this, Ezra? I ain't got 'em. They're of no interest to me,' Marlin lied.

'Of course, they wouldn't be, Marlin,' Ezra said facetiously, 'but they could be of interest to some of the people here, those who are permanent residents or contemplating taking up that status?'

'An' why would that group of people be interested?' Marlin queried.

'To try and force the governor to hold a county seat election, of course,' Ezra replied. 'If the Cove won, it would certainly help justify their investment in this place. The problem with that as a strategy, of course, is that the governor would never give in to such illegal, corrupt methods of persuasion.'

'Well, I guess there may be some logic and truth in what you say,' Marlin reasoned. 'If there is anything I can do to help you, all you have to do is ask.'

'I would like to be able to talk with the miners' leaders, in fact as many of the miners themselves as possible,' Ezra said, seizing the opportunity being offered. 'I wondered if a meeting could be held with, say, fifty miners' representatives, just to let them know the seriousness of this situation, and if they do know what has happened, to come forward in the next forty-eight hours, as an amnesty will be granted.'

'Let me talk to Conway MacPherson,' Marlin proposed. 'Yer know, I don't talk to the miners much myself. They're a unique breed an' you have to know how to handle 'em. Conway's a big brawny Cornishman. He is my eyes, ears and mouthpiece when it comes to the miners. He understands 'em and he also understands me. I'll summon him, an' then he an' I'll jest need five minutes alone, OK?'

'OK,' Ezra agreed. 'Thanks, that's fine.'

★　★　★

'It's on, Ezra,' said Marlin as he came back into the room. 'Eight o'clock this evening in the dance hall downstairs. Fifty miners. Can't get all of the leaders, but the ones that will be there will relay your message back.'

'Thanks,' said Ezra. 'Thanks very much.'

'But,' said Marlin. Ezra looked up, partially surprised and partially annoyed, at what was inevitably going to be some compromising condition or caveat. 'You come from the eastern seaboard, don't yer?'

'Yes,' said Ezra proudly, half wondering the question's relevance. 'We came here to support the pioneers and invest in the widening of the frontier.'

'That's fancy speak for wantin' to make money, jest like everybody else, or in the case of you old aristocrats, makin' even more money. Be careful with that kind of fancy talk, if yer wanna build a rapport with your audience,' Marlin warned. 'The miners' political philosophy is at the opposite end of the spectrum from yours.'

'How?' Ezra asked, puzzled that his fine credentials were not seen as being above challenge.

'You see, the opening of the frontier makes men more equal,' Marlin explained. 'With determination, anybody can go and fin' their fortune, and many have. And with that comes great democratic expectations. There is no longer a need for a man to be subordinate to the ways of the aristocrats from across the Atlantic, who settled in the east.'

'But the people of the east have brought law and order, making the frontier a safer place!' Ezra exclaimed.

'Eventually,' said Marlin. 'Unfortunately, the pioneers often don't have time to wait for the slow wheels of justice to turn. As you ought to know, if a crime's been committed, the victim needs justice to be meted out quickly and effectively before the perpetrator gets away, which is frequently long before the custodians of your law an' order arrive to investigate. You jest need to be aware that many of the people you will be talkin' to, see the world differently from you. So be careful how you put your message across.' And that's why we all think they stole the county records, on your behalf and need to be brought to book, Ezra thought to himself.

★　★　★

Ezra surveyed his audience as they assembled in the dance hall of the Grand Hotel. Rough-looking men, many of them, but serious-looking as well. There was no hint of anger or cynicism, or any form of prejudgment; they just wanted to listen and understand whatever it was they were going to be told.

'Thank you for coming, gentlemen!' Ezra opened full of confidence, knowing that his superior background and knowledge would soon have these men on his side. He explained that a serious criminal offence had taken place, with the illegal removal of the records from Russen but how, out of a gesture of goodwill, an amnesty was being offered to avoid the need for the state governor to call in the National Guard. When he was finished, Ezra was greeted with a deafening silence. 'Thoughts, comments, gentlemen?' he asked, seeking some sort of positive engagement with his speech. Slowly, one miner stood up.

'Are you sayin' we done it?' he asked.

'No, not at all,' Ezra responded firmly. 'But clearly someone has done it, and we have to start somewhere.'

'So have you been to Faux-Port?' someone else asked.

'No, not as yet.'

'Why not! When yer goin' there, mister or don't yer think they done it?'

'I will go there in good time,' Ezra

lied, sensing an animosity arising towards him.

'But yer only got forty-eight hours, mister! Yer told us that yerself,' someone shouted from the back of the hall.

'An' what about a reward, mister. How much is the reward?'

'There isn't a financial reward, if that's what you mean. The reward for the individuals that committed the crime is the amnesty. For everybody else, it's not having to suffer the imposition of the National Guard.'

'Well, clearly these papers or whatever they are, aren't of any financial value then, if there's no monetary reward!' The assembled throng laughed and jeered.

'And that's 'cos this patronising easterner, who thinks he's better than us, can only offer us penalties, not incentives. Typical!' The angry man stood up, waving his fist at Ezra.

'You think we done it, don't yer mister?' A few more men jumped to their feet.

'But you've no evidence to support that, have yer?' shouted another angry man.

'Well, if you think about it logically, the Cove may want to, er, force the governor's hand, to call a county seat election because, being the most populated area in the county, they could win it!' Ezra felt himself sweating as he spoke.

'In the words of your kind, that is circumstantial evidence!' And just to reinforce the point of social differences, the speaker spat in Ezra's face.

'It's far worse than that!' Another miner came forward, his face red with anger. 'It's utter speculation with no solid evidence to go on!' A gang of men came forward and surrounded Ezra. He started to feel scared.

'You came here thinking we was inferior, didn't yer, mister, an' that you knows best? You were tryin' to frighten us off, but have actually ended up insulting our dignity. Get 'im, boys!' Ezra felt himself lifted off the ground and hoisted on to the shoulders of a group of men at the centre of the baying mob. To a mixture of jeering and cheering he was taken out of the dance hall and carried up the street to an old oak tree. As he saw the rope slung over a thick, low-hanging branch, he felt a damp warmth inside his pants.

Ezra was stood up on a wooden chair and his hands tied behind his back. Tears in his eyes, he looked up as he felt the noose drop over his neck and the slack of the rope being taken up. He looked pleadingly towards the face at the top floor window of the Grand Hotel. It was Marlin Bart, surveying the scene below as he puffed on his cigar, a glass of whiskey in his other hand. The last thing Ezra was conscious of was the sound of the fourth bullet separating the last leg from the seat of the chair he was standing on. Fortunately for him, he passed out at that point and was unaware of the increase in pressure as the noose tightened around his neck, breaking it within seconds.

★ ★ ★

'Should they have gone that far?' Conway said to Marlin, as they watched Ezra Danneville's body being cut down from the oak tree.

'I warned Danneville that he could be inviting problems, but clearly he didn't listen. Anyway, it's difficult to stop vigilantes, when they're hell bent on carryin' out justice frontier style,' Marlin pointed out. 'You certainly wouldn't be allowed to stop capital punishment being carried out under Danneville's system of legal justice, so I don't see much difference meself.'

5

William Peters couldn't help but look smug as the train pulled slowly into his home station. He stood up and pulled his case down from the luggage rack. His trip to Washington had gone very well. Not only had he met President Cleveland, but he had sat next to him at the gala dinner. He felt that with his particular blend of intelligent conversation and charm, he had made a good impression on the president.

'My darling!' he exclaimed, as he climbed down the steps of the train. 'You shouldn't have come to pick me up. You know the doctor said that you should get as much rest as possible. Why didn't you send one of the servants?'

'I had to come myself,' his short, portly wife said. She was out of breath and had to briefly stop talking in order to compose herself. 'I'm OK,' she went on, 'but things have turned bad in Holmbury County. First, the county seat records have been stolen. Floyd Greenburn's been put in charge of that investigation, but it's Ezra Danneville! He's . . . he's . . . been murdered in Grainger's Cove. Hung by a vigilante group! He was offering a forty-eight-hour amnesty to whoever had taken the records if they returned them intact.' She wiped a tear from her eye. 'Are you going to call in the National Guard?' William threw his case into the back of the buckboard and climbed on to the seat, taking the reins from his wife. Fortunately the state governor was one of that small group of people who are good in a crisis, focusing quickly and able to make a speedy but objective assessment of their options.

'No,' he said. 'At least, not yet. I made a good impression on the president and I'm not gonna let this episode spoil that. There are other options. Extending the deadline on that amnesty is the first one, but the second one is appointing a new mayor for Russen, one whose methods may be a little unorthodox but which get results, an' I know just the man! Can you sit tight for a few minutes? I need to go back to the platform and send a few messages using the wire service and the pony express.' His red-eyed wife nodded obediently.

★　★　★

The Greenburn sawmill and lumber company provided work for the vast majority of the two thousand people who lived in Denton. Floyd was watching the logs slide down the flume and into the sawmill at the bottom of the hillside, when he received the governor's message by pony express.

'What's it say, boss?' Russ asked.

'The governor's extending Danneville's forty-eight-hour amnesty to seventy-two hours. He's also announcin' that there will be a county seat election, and is offerin' a reward of

$1,000 for any information that leads to the return of the records. He's copied Marlin Bart on it and the Rousseau family in Faux-Port.'

'Mm. There ain't nothin' anyone can do about Ezra's hangin', though, an' that includes the governor,' Russ said philosophically. 'Nobody will have seen anythin', thick as thieves, those miners in the Cove. Don't make it right, either, offerin' a free pardon to someone who's committed a crime.'

'True, but holding a county seat election is probably the right thing to do. And,' Floyd said with enthusiasm, 'an extended deadline and a reward might loosen some tongues regardin' the whereabouts of those records we've been asked to find. What's more, I think I know someone who jest might be able to help us!'

★　★　★

Kittie Rousseau was busy in her kitchen when she received the message from the state governor. 'Michel' she called out to her husband, who was busy attending his tomato plants in the field next to the house. 'Message from the state governor addressed to you.' Michel Rousseau put down his hoe and walked back to the house. The Rousseaux were the largest of the market garden families in the small town of Faux-Port. The town's population of under eighteen hundred made it the smallest community in the county, with many of the residents being immigrant farmers from Europe. Faux-Port's location afforded it a micro-climate making it possible for these immigrant families to grow certain fruits and vegetables that were not available elsewhere. With a ready market in Russen, just across the river, life had worked out well for these people.

'What does it say, Michel?' Kittie asked expectantly.

'Oh, it's nothin' that will interest our people. There's going to be a county seat election, we're too small to win that, and oh, there's going to be an extension to that amnesty and a reward regarding that robbery business in Russen.'

'Ah,' said Kittie, disappointed that the message contained nothing more interesting.

★　★　★

'Read that, Conway,' said Marlin Bart, passing the governor's message to the naïve but influential Cornishman. Marlin paused to give Conway, whose reading skills were limited, time to read the message. 'Still think we were wrong to take them records? Told yer we'd get what we wanned.'

'We gonna hand 'em back an' get the reward money?' Conway asked.

'No. Not for $10,000 dollars, let alone $1,000. I've had 'em safely stashed away an' they might as well stay here, cos that's where they're gonna end up once we win that county seat election.'

64

'D'yer think we're gonna win it?' Conway asked, sounding surprised.

'No doubt about it,' replied Marlin, tapping the side of his nose with his index finger. 'You an' I jest gotta work out the fine details of how!'

★ ★ ★

'Our lives have become totally entwined, haven't they, Ervine?' William Peters remarked as they sat in the governor's private dining room at his country ranch. 'Like the opposite poles of a magnet, we can't keep away from each other.

'When I got that wire from you yesterday,' said Ervine Fulbeck, 'I thought, here we go again, no peace for the wicked, more of Bill's dirty work. So what is it this time?'

'Don't sound so resigned to your fate, Ervine. I know that in your more reflective moments you think I'm heartless. But that just ain't so, Ervine. True, I don't let sentiment stand in the way of achievement, never have done. You only get one real chance in life to achieve greatness, and to show my gratitude towards you, I'm about to offer you yours. I need a new mayor at Russen. It's yours, initially on a short-term probationary period, but if it works out, on a permanent basis. What d'yer say?' Ervine looked shocked. Although he had become wealthy, it was all from ill-gotten gains, and he had longed to free his neck from that particular yoke.

'I . . . I dunno what to say, Bill,' Ervine stammered. 'Yes, of course I'll take it. Are there any strings attached?'

'Yes, of course there are strings attached,' William replied indignantly. 'You've worked for me for long enough not to have to ask me that. I want you to find that damned chest with those county seat records in it.'

'That's gonna be like lookin' for a needle in a haystack, ain't it?' Ervine remarked.

'Maybe, but I can give you the name

of someone who I suspect might make that job a lot easier for you. Her name's Marietta. Holmbury County is a tinderbox, and the town that could set it alight is Grainger's Cove in the form of a county seat war. I have two main sources of information as regards what is happening there. The direct one is Marlin Bart, who will happily give you a censored version, tailored to promote his own agenda. But I have an indirect one which comes to me, although she does not know it, through Marietta. Helps me understand what is really happening on the ground and to validate what Bart is telling me.'

William walked across the room to the fireplace and removed a portrait of himself that was hanging above the mantelpiece, to reveal a small wall safe. He took out a roll of $10 bills — $200 in total — and gave them to Ervine.

'Information costs money — you'll need to pay for it.'

'But that's only a fifth of the reward

money being offered?' Ervine pointed out.

'If Marietta can help she won't wanna be associated with the reward money. Too risky. She could be seen as a blower. But likewise, you as the new mayor of Russen cannot afford to be seen associating with her. You will need to have men with you who can be trusted to negotiate with her, on your behalf. And one last thing, Ervine . . . '

'What's that, boss?' Ervine Fulbeck asked.

'This conversation never happened.'

6

There were only two practical routes to travel to the top of Grainger's Cove from Denton. The first was directly east across the river and straight into the cove itself. Once moored in the small harbour, a mule could be hired to make the steep climb to the top of the gorge and the mine shafts there. Alternatively, if horses were the preferred mode of transport, it was far easier to take the other route and head south along the riverside trail past Faux-Port and cross the River Russen, using the rope ferry, before heading north. Although crossing straight into the cove was more direct and often more practical if the cargo was heavy equipment, transporting a horse-drawn wagon to the top of the gorge was far easier via the rope ferry. Also, if a quick getaway was necessary from the top of the gorge, then horses were always going to be the preferred mode of transport.

Floyd, Chancy and Russ decided to hedge their bets. If they managed to find the missing chest with its archived seals, ledgers and other important documents of government activity, then everything else being equal, a boat would be the quickest way to return. However, smuggling a chest down the gorge to the boat could be difficult, and it would be far easier to conceal it in a covered wagon. Also, if they had to abandon their quest because the locals were on to them and angry, then horseback would enable the fastest getaway.

Consequently, Chancy agreed to row a boat across, while Floyd and Russ took the horses and a wagon via the rope ferry — thus they were prepared for either scenario.

★   ★   ★

'So, Chancy, where would you hide this damned chest, if it were you?' Floyd

70

asked, having left Russ on the top of the gorge to mind the wagon and horses.

'Roun' here?' said Chancy pondering on the question. 'Disused mine shaft. Must be a few of 'em up there, buried in the limestone roof of the gorge.'

'That's my guess too,' Floyd replied.

'We could start with the claims office before we head up to the top, to meet Russ. If we're lucky they might have a record of lapsed claims, an' if we're really lucky they may have mapped 'em! What d'yer think?'

'Yer know, I'd see that as a last resort option. I reckon this place is expanding far too rapidly for those pen pushers in the claims office to keep up with current claims, let alone lapsed ones.'

'So, where d'yer suggest we look first, boss?' Chancy asked. 'Didn't you say you knew someone who might be able to help us?'

'I did,' said Floyd. 'I suggest first we go an' see Miss Molly — but I warn yer she don't work in no claims office!' he added winking at Chancy. 'If Molly don't know exactly what's goin' down, then she can normally put yer on to somebody that does!'

★   ★   ★

Molly's Place stood out in the Cove because it was one of only a handful of two-storey wooden buildings. It was very inferior looking when compared with Marlin Bart's three-storey Grand Hotel, but a virtual palace in terms of comfort and facilities when measured against the dozens of sailcloth tents that surrounded it.

'Floyd Greenburn!' Molly exclaimed, hugging Floyd as he reached the top step of the entrance. 'How are you?' An exuberant, trim woman in her early fifties, Miss Molly greeted Floyd with warmth and affection. 'You an' your friend come into the parlour while I go and call for a bottle of whiskey.' Chancy looked enquiringly at Floyd.

'Molly used to run a small sportin' establishment for the transient labour I employed when we carved out the riverside trail between Faux-Port and Denton,' Floyd said discreetly. 'Surprisin' how many punters bank their confidences with sportin' ladies, but they do. I guess for some, they see the vulnerability as makin' 'em appear human not only to the ladies but to themselves.'

'An' for others, they believe it makes 'em look important in the eyes of the ladies,' Chancy said laughing.

'Like a good banker takes deposits so he can offer profitable loans to the right kind of customers, a good madam can select certain bits of information she gleans from some of her customers, and offer it to other customers who might be seeking it, provided, in her assessment, they are very discreet and able to pay for it,' Floyd continued. 'Now, as I got Miss Molly started in this game with the building of the riverside trail, so my account with her is very much in credit, and I think we might get a quicker result this way, than through the claims office.' Chancy nodded in agreement.

'So, boys,' said Molly, returning with a bottle of whiskey and three glasses. 'What brings yer to town? What can I do for yer?' As Molly poured the drinks, Floyd explained that they were there to try and recover the stolen chest.

'Ah, I thought yer might be,' said Molly, knowingly. 'Official business, then. Right, let's see. First of all, I've no idea personally where it is, but I know of someone who might.' Floyd leaned forward attentively.

'There's a girl who's been working the cribs for about twelve months now. A siren by all accounts, and ambitious. She's the sort of gal that men fall instantly in love with. It sounds like she's got somethin' lucrative goin' on with the bankin' side of her business, which Marlin would probably want to destroy, at least in the longer term once he had milked it fer himself. Fortunately for Marietta, he rarely takes girls from the cribs if he needs more staff for the Grand — he'd rather import a more up-market product. She deals a lot with the new miners, those who've jest arrived, an' don't know the set-up. They call her the deal maker, cos she puts those boys who wanna buy a claim quickly in touch with a seller. She knows what claims are good an' what ones ain't worth botherin' with, an' who's a scammer an' who isn't.

'But some folk say she's turnin' into a deal breaker, an' that's cos she's getting greedy. Tryin' to realize her financial ambitions too quickly, an' not checkin' her buyers' credentials properly. Yer can get away with that now an' again, but keep doin' it, an' one day you'll double cross Mr Nasty — an' when she does that, then that'll be her lot.'

'An' where do we find this woman, Molly?' Floyd asked.

'Walk up the street towards the end of the Cove where most of the cribs are, an' jest ask for Marietta.'

'Thanks, Molly.'

'That's all right, Floyd. I owe yer a few for what yer done fer me in the past.'

* * *

'So boys, how d'yer like yer fun?' Marietta stood in the middle of her tent, legs astride and hands on hips, her dark wavy hair flowing over her shoulders.

'We're not here for fun,' said Floyd coming straight to the point. 'We want information.' Marietta moved slowly towards him in a seductive fashion and jabbed her index finger into the tin star on his chest.

'It says, 'Deputy State Marshal'. Sounds like official business, Mr Marshal,' she said.

'Yep. It's about this wooden chest of stolen county seat records — d'yer know anythin' about that?'

'Might do,' Marietta replied, looking Floyd directly in the eye. 'Depends

76

exactly what it is yer wanna know, Mr Marshal.'

'We wanna know where it's been hidden.'

'Do yer, now? Well, that'll cost yer a hundred dollars.'

'We ain't got a hundred dollars on us right now. If you tell us where it is an' it's actually there, we'll come back with your money.'

'Yer worried I'd lie to yer an' skip town for $100, are yer?'

'I promise, on my word as a deputy state marshal, we'll be back.'

'Huh, the local preacher man promised that if I behaved like a good gal, I wouldn't end up as no whore.'

'He was probably right.'

'He was probably wrong, mister. Good gal behaviours don't pay the rent, or buy a gal any financial independence. Yer still have to suck up to some dude, an' that's jest whorin' for free, in my book.'

'That's cynical in mine,' Floyd said, sparring with her. Marietta ignored him. She was more interested in the tin star on Floyd's chest. She moved forward and removed it.

'Here's the deal,' she said. 'I tell yer where the chest is an' you go get it. If yer don't come back with my $100 by nightfall, your badge will be sent to the state governor with an anonymous note tellin' 'im that you lost it offerin' it as a bribe for information. Governor Peters ain't gonna be impressed. He'd realize that if it wasn't for the honesty of the model citizen who returned it, this tin star could have ended up in the hands of a two-bit gunslinger who wanted to carry out an easy bank job. Now what d'yer say, Mr Greenburn?'

'So yer know who I really am, then.'

''Course I do. I knew all along. It was easy to work out. You boys might not have wanted yer fun right now, but I always like to have mine. I was jest toyin' with yer.'

'It's a deal,' said Floyd. 'I trust yer.'

★   ★   ★

'Yer don't think she's cheated on us, do yer, Floyd?' Chancy asked, looking despondent. They had been looking for the disused mine shaft that supposedly contained the stolen chest for nearly an hour now.

'We must be in the right area,' said Floyd thoughtfully. 'There's a number of blocked up entrances aroun' here, but none are marked with that damned symbol she mentioned.'

'They must have all been diggin' in an' aroun' the same seam but I guess it gave out. How did she describe that symbol again?' Russ asked.

'Not very well, to be honest. She said it was a circle, with some sort of mark on it.' Floyd answered.

'The Craven cattle family's brand was a circle with a cross overlaid on it,' said Russ. 'They were local rich cattle drovers, but when the cattle drives stopped passing through Russen, rumour has it that they invested nearly all their wealth up here in the gorge lookin' for gold an' damn

79

well lost it all, as well. Look, let's go back to the trail an' start agen,' he said scrambling over the rocks and small boulders.

'OK,' said Chancy. 'So you come up here, with this heavy chest that you've stolen. Now, the temptation would be to hide it in one of the shafts furthest away from the trail, but you'd have to carry it over some pretty rough ground, an' when you look through the gaps in the wood that's been crudely used to seal off the mine, many of these shafts don't look safe. Marlin Bart's too shrewd an operator to risk hiding his loot somewhere where it could be permanently buried if the shaft caved in.'

'I get you,' said Russ with a note of optimism in his voice. 'So, the implication is you'd prefer to drag it jest off the trail if possible. And the Cravens had money, so they probably built a safe, solid shaft or series of shafts.'

'You're right, boys,' shouted out Floyd. 'I've found it over here, jest to the side of the trail. The symbol has virtually worn off the wood.' He grabbed an axe and started to hack down the rough wooden planks that blocked the entrance. Within a yard of the entrance the shaft dropped vertically into the ground, a gaping dark hole. Floyd threw some pebbles down the hole and listened as they hit the bottom. 'I'd guess that's about twenty feet deep but there was no noise of a splash, so it must be dry down there. Let's get some rope. Chancy, you stay guard here at the top while Russ an' I climb down. Looks promising.'

★   ★   ★

Marietta weighed up the two rough-looking men standing in front of her. One looked quite ugly, with a gaunt face and a large nose, features that he couldn't do anything about — but he could have bothered to shave. He could probably also have avoided losing his two front teeth, and almost certainly

81

prevented the remaining ones from discolouring to the degree that they had. His companion was slightly better looking but had very cold eyes and a permanent sly grin plastered across his face.

'You, Marietta?' the ugly one said. She nodded. 'Well, we wan' somethin' from yer.'

'Most men do,' Marietta replied, 'What exactly do you boys wan'?'

'Information, honey,' the one with the sly grin said. 'We unnerstan' yer might know the whereabouts of this stolen chest containin' the Russen county seat records.'

'Who tol' yer that, mister?'

'Oh, one of our contacts. If yer information is good, we'll pay yer well for it.'

'How much is well?' Marietta asked.

'$100.'

'Not enough, mister. Yer see, that chest is mighty popular. There's been others sniffin' aroun' here today lookin fer that.

'Is that so?' said 'Sly grin'. 'What about $200, shall we say all inclusive?' Marietta thought quickly. She didn't like to double deal, but this was too good a chance to miss — easy money. If the marshal were to find out that he'd been double crossed he'd put his disappointment down to the fact that he'd trusted a whore. If these boys felt she'd double crossed them, they'd probably kill her. And the marshal and his lackey would be no match for 'Ugly' and 'Sly grin' if they met up. A part-time deputy marshal against professional gun slingers? No contest. Besides, she deliberately hadn't been over helpful with the detail of her directions, half hoping that Marshal Greenburn might go down the wrong shaft and get lost, missing their nightfall deadline. Marietta was quite confident she could sell his tin star for a lot more than the $100 she had agreed Floyd should pay her for the information she'd given him.

'It's a deal,' she said offering 'Sly

grin' her hand to shake. He took it and pulled her towards him. She felt the stubble on his face prick her cheek and smelt the whiskey on his breath as he tried to kiss her.

'You guys had better get goin',' she said pushing him away with her other hand. 'Those boys who were hangin' aroun' earlier gotta coupler hours start on yer.'

'Oh, don't worry about 'em,' said 'Sly grin'. 'We won't be long with yer.'

7

'You hit the ground yet, Floyd?' Russ shouted down the shaft. Floyd looked up towards the daylight. He could see Russ's face leaning over the side of the shaft.

'Yep. There's an iron ladder layin' on the ground down here. I think it's fer climbin' down this first bit of the shaft which I came down by rope. Hold on. I'm gonna try and see if I can rig it up.' He hauled the ladder up in stages, periodically resting it against the rock face.

'OK. You can come on down now.'

'Good sign,' said Russ as he climbed on to the ladder. 'Suggests this shaft might still be in use, but they didn't wanna make it easy for jest anyone to climb down.' Floyd waited until Russ stepped off the bottom of the ladder.

'There's an iron railtrack on the

floor,' Russ said thoughtfully. 'Would make it easy to move a chest,' he exclaimed, 'if there was a wagon!' Floyd used his cigar to light the lantern they had brought with them. 'An' there it is!' Russ pointed thirty yards along the railroad to where it was just possible to make out a small drop-side wagon.

'These Cravens really did mean business!' said Floyd as he held the lantern steady at arm's length to light up the tunnel as much as possible. The two men stopped talking and stared at the flame. Burning upright, they noticed it occasionally flicked back towards the entrance shaft.

'There's a draft from further along the tunnel,' Russ said. 'Must open up somehow to the outside.' After they had passed the wagon, it became easier to walk along the track itself, since for most of the way the width of the tunnel was only slightly wider than that of the wagon. The spruce props that prevented the ceiling caving in were sturdy and made of good timber.

'The Cravens must have really thought they were on to somethin' here, given the time and effort they must have put into building this,' Floyd remarked. 'Must have found some gold up here, in this particular vein, otherwise why make this kind of investment?' They paused as they passed some small galleries off to either side of the railtrack.

'Yet these galleries go no real distance at all. And they smell slightly damp,' Russ observed. 'They must have been very disappointed every time they attempted to branch off and dug deeper and deeper into the rock.' They continued to follow the railroad as it snaked its way through the dark, descending very slightly for another hundred yards or so — and then, as they rounded what turned out to be the last bend, the warm air became cooler, breezier even, and daylight started to brighten the tunnel. Fifty yards ahead a metal grill blocked off the end of the tunnel, but through its vertical metal bars it was possible to make out the forested slopes on the west side of the River Russen. And beneath the grill, Floyd and Russ spotted their prize: a small chest, loosely covered in a piece of sailcloth. But at the same moment they heard the sound of Chancy's whistle — their predetermined alarm call! The echo of the tunnel gave it an eerie, almost ominous sound.

Floyd hurried to the end of the tunnel to assess the situation. Looking down through the grill he could see the smooth shoreline below, probably a couple of hundred feet drop, but where it would be possible to moor their boat. Looking up he could see a winch wheel arrangement protruding from the rock face. The Cravens had obviously used this as a way of transporting equipment up from the river, then along the railtrack.

'We can get out here if this grill will open,' Floyd said to Russ. 'We'll need all the rope from the wagon to lower the chest, but we should have enough. Chancy will need to bring the boat around. Go an' see why he's soundin' the alarm call. It's probably cos someone's comin', but you an' he will have to decide what to do. I'm gonna try an' get this grill open.'

* * *

'What's the problem, Chancy?' Russ asked as he climbed out of the shaft into the daylight.

'Take a look,' said Chancy, offering Russ the telescope.

'Damn. Four riders. One looks like a woman. Could be Marietta, but difficult to say from this distance. They've passed the point where all the active mines are, so why are they still ridin' this way?'

'I reckon they're about three-quarters of a mile away, but the rough terrain will slow 'em down — realistically, they're probably thirty minutes away, at the most.'

'We've found the chest, an' Floyd is confident we can lower it down by rope through what is basically a large hole in the cliff face, to the shore. It would mean yer havin' to go an' get the boat an' bring it round. What d'yer think?'

'Time is precious. I back Floyd's judgement. We're not gonna be able to bring the chest down past those riders without them questionin' what we're doin'. Woman or not, I don't like the look of any of 'em. Takin' the chest out by the river is the only way.'

'What do we do with the horses an' the wagon?'

'I'll leave the horses in the livery at the top of the cove, when I go to get the boat. As for the wagon, let's turn it over an' try an' make it look abandoned. If we can use it to cover over the Cravens' branding sign, it might buy us a bit more time, if these riders are really after us.'

★　★　★

Ervine Fulbeck sat last in line of the four riders as they made their way slowly up to the top of the gorge. In front of him was 'Sly grin', followed by the woman, Marietta, who had her hands tied together but with a scarf hanging loosely over her wrists and the reins, so as not to attract any unwanted attention from the miners they passed. At the head of this small procession was 'Ugly', whose exceptionally mean look betrayed his mood.

Fulbeck was angry with his two male companions, and they knew it. He had told them what to do to get the information out of the woman and feel confident that she was telling the truth. First, offer her the money, he had said, then one of them must stay with her while the other one validates her story. If her story doesn't check out, then just beat the truth out of her — but, he had warned them, never, ever take the woman prisoner as an insurance against her lying and force her to come with us. And the reason, as far as he was concerned, was plain common sense: the new mayor of Russen could not afford to have this woman spread malicious rumours about him or, in the worst case, start blackmailing him.

It now meant that, whether she was telling the truth or not, she would have to be done away with. And Fulbeck had learnt from experience that it was always best if the victim appeared to have totally disappeared. Vanished, as it were, into thin air. No trace of the body meant no solid evidence — the difference between having a noose put around your neck and living to fight another day. He shuddered at the agony he continued to live through, wondering if someone was going to uncover some of his past mistakes and put two and two together.

'You OK back there, boss?' 'Sly grin' shouted, turning around in his saddle, hoping that Fulbeck had calmed down. 'Shuddup, idiot!' Ervine shouted back. These fools plainly didn't understand the problems they had created him. For men of brawn, capturing the woman and taking back the $200 dollars they had paid her, represented brains — clever thinking. Now, whether they found the chest or not, Fulbeck was going to have to find a way of disposing of her body where it couldn't be found. The best bet at the moment was probably a disused mine shaft, but it would mean finding one that was easy to open yet deep enough to deter anyone from wanting to venture too far inside. If this woman was to go missing, assuming that someone really wanted to find her, a disused mine shaft would be the obvious place to start looking.

★   ★   ★

'Is it budgin'?' Russ asked. Floyd wiped the sweat from his brow and once again hit the lock on the grill with the piece of rock in his hand.

'No, it ain't,' he replied. 'Too well made. Exactly the same problem with the hinges. We're gonna have to shoot the lock off to get this grill to swing open. I'm frightened the noise will attract attention but we'll jest have to risk it.'

'We'll make it one of the last things we do. Let's feed the rope between the top edge of the grill and the rock face and over the pulley wheel. Then if we can thread it back, we can tie the chest on the end. Once Chancy appears with the boat we can shoot the lock off and lower away.'

'Good idea,' said Floyd. 'An' since that clever bitch took my badge there's no longer any need to let anyone who sees us recognize who we are. Let's cover our faces. If we pull this off, I might wanna be a bit nosey and look inside this chest, which would make it unofficial business.' Within ten minutes they had the chest tied on and ready to be lowered, the rope being fed over a ceiling joist and tied securely to the base of a pit prop, inside the mine shaft.

'There's Chancy,' Russ said, pointing down to the river. 'He's tying the boat up now. Let's go!' It took two shots with the Winchester to blow the lock free, but once that was done, the grill swung inwards on its hinges and Russ and Floyd were able to push the chest out into the open air. It dropped slightly, as its weight enabled the slack to be taken up, swung gently backwards and forwards before finally coming to rest, suspended in mid-air and ready to be lowered down to the ground.

★　★　★

'Where d'yer reckon those shots came from, boss?' 'Ugly' asked. 'Sounded funny.'

'Near here but underground,' Ervine replied, full of contempt for the man's inability to come up with a reasonable explanation himself. He looked around him, carefully surveying the landscape. 'That wagon over there,' he said pointing at the overturned wagon which Russ and Chancy had left behind. 'Don't look natural. Go and move it,' he ordered. 'Sly grin' and 'Ugly' tied a rope from their horses to the base of the wagon and pulled it back on to its wheels. It was then easy to push it out of the way.

'The entrance to this shaft has been tampered with,' 'Sly grin' said.

'Yeah, an' there's that symbol. The circle with the cross overlaid,' 'Ugly' exclaimed.

'I told yer I was tellin' the truth, so can I go now?' Marietta pleaded. 'Yer can keep yer lousy $200!'

'Not so fast, lady. We ain't found the chest, yet.' 'Sly grin' gave her a menacing look. 'Shall we see if it's here?'

★   ★   ★

'D'yer hear that,' whispered Russ. 'Someone's got into the shaft.' Floyd dowsed the flame of the lantern and looked out of the large gap in the rock face, where they had removed the metal grill.

'Go on,' he urged Russ. 'You climb down the rope first an' help Chancy load the chest into the boat. I'll try an' hold 'em off if needs be. If I'm not down by the time you boys are ready to row upstream, then go without me.' Floyd found a crevice in the rock face where he could partially conceal himself but also peer out to see what was going on, on the shoreline below.

Whoever had entered the shaft was being very quiet about their presence. If it was the three male riders and Marietta, she would have double-crossed Floyd. And that wouldn't be surprising, given that the state governor had offered a reward for the return of the county seat records. Every two-bit gunslinger in the state would be making their way here. The odds of getting out alive could turn out to be poor, especially if it was Floyd's six-gun against three professionals packing two pistols each.

Floyd looked down at the shoreline. Russ and Chancy were loading the chest into the boat. He returned his pistol to its holster, stepped back several yards from the edge of the shaft, and took a running jump through the window into the open air. He grabbed hold of the rope, which was dangling from the pulley, and as it swung backwards and forwards, lowered himself down to the shore below. As his feet hit the ground, Russ and Chancy gave him covering fire, pinning back Fulbeck and his two cronies, who were now all masked, away from the ledge. Floyd climbed into the boat and opened fire himself while Russ and Chancy rowed away from the shore.

★   ★   ★

'I'll be damned boss. They got away!' exclaimed 'Ugly'. 'What do we do now?'

'I think the first thing we do is ask Marietta if she knows who they are!' Fulbeck said.

'How would I know who they are?' she retorted angrily. 'They were masked. You saw that!' It was as

Ervine had expected. This cheap, dirty, low-down whore, whose finest achievement in life to date was working the cribs in the tent city of a new mining town, was a damned sight smarter than his own two men.

'You told my boys earlier there were other men lookin' for that damned chest. That weren't them, then?' Ervine asked again.

'Yeah, they were lookin' for the chest as well, 'cos you'd already told 'em where it was,' said 'Sly grin', starting to feel clever as he realized that the boss was trying to catch out Marietta. He stroked the underneath of Marietta's chin with the back of his index finger. 'You haven't been a naughty girl, have yer? You haven't tried to double cross us, have yer?' Ervine pulled 'Sly grin' away from her.

'Yer got her $200 on yer,' he said, 'so you go an' get two small boats from the Cove. Rowin' boats will do. One just big enough to take one person an' one large enough for two people. Bring 'em to the shoreline below.' 'Sly grin' slouched off to carry out his errand, aggrieved at being put down by his boss, who clearly underestimated his clever reasoning.

'Now, let's see, Marietta. It is Marietta, isn't it?' Ervine continued.

'Yes, sir,' she replied, thinking that politeness might work better for her than anger with this seemingly educated man.

'So if you didn't know these men personally, how did you know that we had competition?'

'The tent city is a close community, sir. Word travels fast. I told you because I thought it right an' proper to make you aware. A sportin' lady learns many things about other people's business — many are confidences that we keep to ourselves, but there's the odd occasion where it's morally right to share.' Ervine tried not to show his irritation, but this girl was starting to lay it on a bit thick if she believed that her credentials gave her the right to make moral judgements.

'And did the closeness of your community inform you as to what they did, what their interest in the chest was?' he asked.

'Oh, they were nobodies. Opportunists after a quick buck. Certainly not in the same league as yourself, Mr Fulbeck.' She felt that this approach would save her from any nasty fate that Ervine Fulbeck might be planning, since in her experience courtesy, flattery and subordination to one's betters was normally a trump card. But if Ervine had any doubts about showing Marietta mercy, it was that card which did for her.

'Damn,' Ervine muttered to himself. 'She does know who I am!'

★   ★   ★

It was dusk when 'Sly grin' returned with the boats and met up with his two companions on the eastern shore of the River Russen. They moved quickly.

101

Marietta was gagged and bound with stones and rocks tied into her clothing. She was bundled into the smaller boat which was pushed out into the south-flowing current, and the boat was then holed just below the waterline by two bullets. 'Ugly' was commanded by Fulbeck to go back to the top of the gorge and bring their horses back to Russen, while 'Sly grin' was to row Ervine back to Russen.

As they approached the small group of rocks in the middle of the river which divided the river into two separate navigation channels, their boat started to overtake the smaller one, which was now beginning to take on water. Ervine Fulbeck asked 'Sly grin' to hold their craft steady, and raised his Winchester to his shoulder, aligning the sights on the helpless Marietta. Then without saying a word, he lowered the rifle and laid it to rest on his lap.

'I wonder if we should show this poor soul some mercy,' he said, turning to look at 'Sly grin'. 'Tell me honestly.

What do you think?' Somewhat taken aback by the nature of the question, 'Sly grin' raised the oars and let the boat move through the water under its own momentum.

'No, boss,' he said in a quiet but menacing voice. Ervine raised an eyebrow.

'An' why not?' he asked.

'Because she done us, boss,' 'Sly grin' said loudly, his anger erupting. 'That whore done us over!'

8

'No sign of Marietta,' Chancy said. 'I've asked various people in the Cove an' in the tent city. Been missin' twenty-four hours now.'

'She's either done a runner or is lyin' dead somewhere,' Floyd replied. 'Got my tin star supposedly as well.'

'Gonna report it lost?' asked Russ.

'No, not jest yet. Least not until we've handed this chest back. I might get a replacement knocked up. I sense this Marietta episode isn't over yet.'

'We still plannin' to take the chest back tonight?' Chancy asked.

'Yep,' Floyd said. 'We're gonna leave it by the steps at the back door of the town hall. Anonymous like. Keep people guessin'. My old soldier's instinct tells me that now is not the right time to lay our cards on the table if we wanna get ahead of the game. Too many strange things happenin' aroun' here. The murders of Adison Marson and Ezra Danneville, now the disappearance of Marietta. Even Sarah Tamswaite's manner suggests that she is hidin' somethin'.'

'May jest be a line of coincidences,' Russ suggested.

'Maybe, but I sense there's more to it than that,' Floyd said. 'Is stealin' the Russen county seat records jest a provocative side show, or does it lie at the centre of all these strange coincidences? Besides, we've risked our lives to get hold of that chest. I'll be damned if I ain't gonna take a peek inside it, before we hand it back.' As they left to go down to the saw mill, Russ and Chancy heard the sound of Floyd's gun being fired as he shot the lock off the chest.

★ ★ ★

The county seat records were all filed in similar sized boxes which fitted neatly inside the chest. After ten minutes of leafing through them, Floyd was starting to get disappointed. File after file seemed to contain either meeting minutes, legal documents or tax collection records. And then, almost as if they had been placed purposefully at the bottom of the chest, he came across a file marked *Holmbury County Civil War Museum — Monthly Returns — Adison Marson*. He flicked through the meticulously kept records of attendance numbers, admission receipts, exhibits which provoked the most interest. Finally, behind those documents there was a section of the file headed *Research*.

Adison Marson's research posed some interesting questions regarding the massacre of a civilian village by the Confederate Army over twenty-five years ago, in neighbouring Honer County. Why, for example, had Captain Travis, the commander in charge of the soldiers who carried out the atrocity, been given a free pardon by the military court? Travis's defence was that he had tried to stop the brutal killings, not start them. If that were so, then why hadn't the army made some attempt to honour such bravery? How was it that Travis had seemingly vanished? As had Captain Emmett Aldstone who, having arrived late on the scene of the carnage, was still able to verify Captain Travis's story to the court, claiming to have seen what happened from afar. Was Aldstone's disappearance just another coincidence?

These unanswered questions by themselves were nothing new to Greenburn. He had lived with the agony they had created ever since his cousin and the other soldiers of Travis's unit were hanged for carrying out the atrocity, but on insufficient and poorly substantiated evidence. The part of Marson's research that really grabbed his attention was the paragraph stating that of the four men under Aldstone's command who were with him at the time, two had mysteriously been murdered, both taking bullets through the forehead — the same death that Adison Marson had suffered, shortly before Floyd Greenburn found him in the water tank, on the night the museum caught fire. Coincidence indeed! If this wasn't enough to whet Floyd's appetite, Adison's unanswered request to the new governor for state funding to verify some new evidence suggesting that Captain Ransom Travis's tombstone lay in a graveyard in the south of Honer County, certainly was.

It was as if, Floyd thought to himself, the only response Adison Marson got for his request to the state governor for research funding, was a bullet through the head. Another coincidence? They were starting to mount up. Floyd decided to hold on to Adison's research file rather than return it with the other records. Not that he needed confirmation of his hunch to return the chest anonymously, but the information that the late Adison Marson had provided him with, made that decision indisputable.

'Floyd!' the Denton town blacksmith exclaimed. He quenched the red-hot metal rod he had been beating into shape on his anvil in the water bucket, and put down his hammer and tongs. 'How yer doin'?'

'I'm fine,' said Floyd. 'And you, Dan?'

'Good, thanks. What can I do for yer?'

'I need a replacement deputy state marshal badge. Can yer knock one up for me?'

'Sure. A tin one?'

'No. I wan' it made of brass, backed with nickel, if yer can, Dan.'

'Ah, a protective, armoured one rather than a decorative one. Sure. Course I can.'

★   ★   ★

It had just turned midnight when Floyd and his two companions tied their boat

109

up alongside a small jetty at Russen and masked their faces with their neckerchiefs. It was a moonless night, which helped in their task of returning the chest to the town hall unseen. Chancy stayed with the boat and its important cargo, while Floyd and Russ agreed to check that their chosen route to the town hall was clear, and that they could operate under the cover of virtually complete darkness.

Everything seemed fine until they reached Sarah Tamswaite's residence, where they saw a figure come skulking out of the garden and disappear into the undergrowth. It was as if whoever it was, was as keen not to be spotted as Floyd and Russ were. Whatever his reasons, the individual's furtive movements made him look suspicious. Floyd signalled to Russ to check the rest of the route while he decided to follow this figure further.

Almost as if he realized he was being followed, the figure worked his way through some back alleys to reach Main

Street. Russ struggled not to lose him, uncertain of places where he could tuck into in order to conceal himself. But once on Main Street and as he approached the door of the most exclusive hotel along there, the man strode forwards more confidently. And as he turned to go up to the front door, the lantern above the door briefly lit up his profile: it was William Peters. Hm, Floyd thought to himself, well, Tuesday night is meeting night for the Temperance Society, and he is the executive trustee, so maybe his movements were not as untoward as perhaps they first appeared.

★   ★   ★

The journey from the jetty to the back door of the town hall was easy and uneventful. Floyd and Chancy carried the chest between them on an old army stretcher consisting of two wooden carrying poles stitched into a bed of sailcloth. Russ acted as scout, checking that the coast was still clear. They deposited the chest to the side of the back door, partially covered by a bush, with the remainder of it covered by the sailcloth stretcher, and then left. There was no reason to linger. No lights went on in any of the surrounding buildings. The neighbourhood was asleep. Apart from one person.

Having got rid of William Peters back to his hotel, Sarah Tamswaite had decided not to light her bedroom lantern before retiring, but to take a reflective look at the dark, expansive world outside her window. She had initially looked expectantly upwards at the heavens, but her gaze had been distracted by three masked men in the street below, carrying what appeared to be a chest or some such luggage on a stretcher. They disappeared into the dark. Sarah maintained her vigil at the window, curious as to what might be happening. Then she let out a slight gasp as they reappeared a short while later, but empty handed, and put her hand to her mouth, as the build and gait of one of them looked remarkably like that of Floyd Greenburn.

9

'So, Mr Bart, sir. I thought you weren't gonna return that chest,' Conway said to Marlin Bart as they walked up the muddy street towards the Grand Hotel.

'An' I didn't,' said Marlin. 'Somebody stole it from us, an' I guess they returned it. Governor Peters is sayin' that Ervine Fulbeck recovered it, an' that's why he's confirmed that Fulbeck's appointment as Mayor of Russen is now permanent.'

'D'yer think that's true?' Conway asked. 'Never heard of a man bein' promoted to mayor for doin' somethin' like that.'

'No. I don't think it's true for a moment. If Fulbeck recovered it, it was from the back door where someone else had left it. Peters was jest lookin' fer a reason to make his man's promotion permanent, that's all.'

'So, who d'yer think put it there?'

'I dunno fer sure, but I would guess it was Floyd Greenburn. He an' his boys were askin' questions around the Cove on the day it went missin' from that shaft where we'd hidden it.'

'Greenburn?' Conway repeated sounding surprised. 'So why wouldn't he own up to doin' that? That's the sort of thing he would normally take credit for, ain't it?'

'I dunno, Conway, but yer certainly startin' to ask the right questions. I'm impressed.' Conway felt pleased with himself. He knew how to mix with and lead his own sort, but he had always felt intellectually inferior to the likes of Marlin Bart. But Conway took pride in his assumption that his leadership skills, his ability to build trust and his intelligence must have been better than that of many of his peers and that was the reason why Marlin Bart paid him so handsomely.

'Is that what yer wanna talk to me about now?' Conway asked, feeling that he was on a bit of an intellectual roll.

'Naw,' replied Marlin. 'I don't wanna talk to you about who stole the chest back off me an' why. But I do wanna talk to you about the consequences of that. So, go on up.' Marlin politely gestured to Conway to ascend the front steps of the Grand Hotel ahead of him. That's another thing I could learn from the boss, Conway thought to himself. Some better manners.

★ ★ ★

The Cornishman sank back into the large leather armchair in Marlin's lounge, and drew on the large cigar his boss had just offered him. Marlin walked back towards him holding an empty glass in one hand and a bottle of whiskey in the other.

'Here, Conway. Here's yer scotch.' He placed the glass on the small round table at the side of the armchair and filled the glass full of neat whiskey. 'Now I don't wan'cha to down that like it's a glass of water, Conway, like yer used to. Yer need to keep yer head straight if yer wanna understand what I am about to tell yer, 'cos yer may need to explain it to yer men.'

'OK, got it, Mr Bart, sir.' Marlin produced a small easel from under his desk and placed it on top. Conway had a clear view of it from where he sat, and realized that this was the real reason Marlin had offered him the luxurious-looking armchair, rather than that he regarded Conway as an honoured guest. Marlin took a piece of chalk from the desk drawer and began writing on the blackboard.

Grainger's Cove 3,000 people 1st
Russen 2,500 people 2nd
Denton 2,000 people 3rd
Faux-Port 1,750 people 4th

'Now,' said Marlin as he perched himself on the corner of the desk. 'These are the key population figures for Holmbury County. The numbers include a few children who won't be eligible to vote in the forthcoming county seat elections obviously, but there ain't enough of them to alter the numbers significantly. So, based on everyone who can vote, votin' for their local community would mean that we'd come first and Faux-Port last. Right?'

'Right, Mr Bart, sir.' Conway agreed. He rewarded himself with a sip of whiskey.

'An' realistically how many towns are really interested in winnin' this seat?'

'One, sir,' Conway replied 'Us.'

'Wrong, Conway. There's two. There's us an' there's Russen, who can't afford to lose it, if they wanna maintain their lifestyles.'

'But they ain't got as many people as us?' Conway pointed out, wondering if he had already missed something clever.

'They could have more if not everyone here turns out to vote.' Marlin paused to let the point sink in. 'So, you're first job is to make sure everybody here votes. Now we know that not everybody's gonna be arsed to turn out, so yer jest might have to fill in ballot papers on their behalf, an' distract the overseers from the other towns, so that yer can sneak those papers into the ballot boxes.'

'I get it, Mr Bart, sir. I get it.' Once again Conway rewarded himself with a sip of whiskey.

'Good,' said Marlin. 'So, now get this!' He picked up the chalk and started scribbling on the blackboard once more.

Russen 2,500 people
Denton <u>2,000</u> people
        4,500

Grainger's Cove 3,000 people
Faux-Port   <u>1,750</u> people
                4,750

'But what about the people from Denton an' Faux-Port, Conway? I'd be surprised if they don't vote, an' I expect most of them will, even though they know they ain't gonna win it. So, who d'yer think the people of Denton are most likely to vote for, Conway?'

'Well, some of 'em will naturally vote for their home town, but a few of 'em might vote fer us. Lumberjacks an' miners both know how to graft fer a livin'. On the other hand, I guess that Greenburn's established law an' order there an' they seem to like it so, probably as you've got it on yer board there, Mr Bart, sir, I reckon' many of 'em will vote fer Russen.'

'Good analysis, Conway! Good analysis!' A few right answers and a little drop of whiskey were working wonders for Conway's confidence.

'But Mr Bart, sir,' he interjected, 'I can't see the people of Faux-Port turnin' out fer us. They're not a bit like us. They make their livin' from the land like most other folk do, but plantin' tomatoes and lettuce is not like diggin' deep into the hard ground. They're far gentler folk than us. We're tough, rugged speculators. The unknown is a challenge for us, not a risk to be avoided. Besides, the main market for their produce is Russen, so I'd think they would vote for them as well.'

'Of their own free will, I'm sure you're right, Conway. But, an' this is what you need to understand, an' I think yer will once I've pointed it out to yer: your words — we're tough, they're gentle. My words — similar to yours — we're strong, they're weak. And when the strong lean on the weak, the weak crumble. Do as they're told. Yer get my meanin'?'

'Yes sir. So if we send a few men over an' lean on 'em, they'll vote fer us, is that it?'

Conway paused as he processed the thought, not without some concern.

'Yer wonderin' how Russen might react, if we do that. Am I right?' Marlin asked.

'Yes,' said Conway still thinking it through. 'I think,' he said hesitantly, 'that they wouldn't wanna get involved?

No, of course they wouldn't,' he suddenly exclaimed with confidence. 'They wouldn't wanna get into a physical fight with us even with the state governor appointing a new 'tough guy' mayor! So yer wan' me to organize a small team to do that?'

'Of course I do, Conway. A little team that can point out the advantages, to the good people of Faux-Port, of voting for the winning side in the county seat election. Winning would mean I would have control not only of the Cove, but of the whole county. People would flock here to invest. They always do, attracted by the power the county seat affords. It'd be very good for me, Conway, which means it would be very good for you, too. But what I am asking you to get your team to do in Faux-Port is man's work. Bad man's work.

'Now we have a lot of miners here who will fight for justice an' do it in an honourable an' courageous way. Basically they are good men, like Floyd

Greenburn. But they will not be suitable for this kind of work. You will need to recruit good men who have turned bad, possibly very bad, past redemption. Not men born bad though, 'cos they are sociopaths, Conway, an' sociopaths don't like takin' orders. No, you'll need to recruit good men turned bad. They don't have to be clever. They need to be able to do what you tell 'em, once I have briefed you. Yer think yer can do that for me?'

'There's a few hangers-on in the Cove who fit that description, Mr Bart, sir. Yes, I think I can do that for yer.'

'Excellent, Conway. I'm so glad that once yer worked it through, yer came to the same conclusion as me. Here.' Marlin said passing Conway the three-quarters full bottle of whiskey. 'Top yer glass up an' finish the bottle.'

Conway sat back in the armchair and allowed himself a brief period of reflection on his circumstances, while savouring the taste of top quality whiskey. A few years ago he would never have seen himself in this position. He was basically a simple man, that honourable and courageous justice fighter that Marlin had described. In fact, coincidentally, Conway had once described himself as a moral idealist but with a temper. Yet the higher he got in the world, the more he began to realize that moral principles and ideals by themselves don't make the world go around. They might still form the basic wheels and cogs of the machine called life, but they would often only turn with the right kind of lubricant, and sometimes, like it or not, that required the use of oils such as bribery, corruption and intimidation. Maybe that meant that he himself was a 'good man turned bad', as Marlin described it. He drained the glass and refilled it, and allowed the whiskey to push that particular thought out of his mind.

10

Apart from market day, which occurred once a week, the small town of Faux-Port normally had an enchanting sleepy atmosphere. The actual centre consisted of a single street with no more than two dozen clapboard-style buildings, painted in various bright colours, lining each side. Most of these were commercial buildings such as the hotel, the saloon, livery, the blacksmith, a small chapel, the newspaper proprietor's office, the store and a number of warehouses. There was no sheriff's office because there was no sheriff. A deputy from Russen would be in attendance on market day, but otherwise the need for an enforcer of law and order had not arisen. In fact, very few people lived in the town. The bulk of the population lived in the rich agricultural hinterland, mainly on small-holdings where the micro climate and various irrigation aids enabled them to grow their market garden produce.

A clear exception to this was the harbour-master, whose two-storey dwelling provided his home on the top floor and his office on the ground floor. This white building was a landmark on the shoreline. Standing on slightly raised ground at the end of the street, close to the jetty, it had long been a navigation aid for river traffic entering Faux-Port's small natural harbour. Market day over for another week and the warehouses emptied of their produce, the harbour-master had little to do but wait for the following week's burst of activity. He spent most of this time either studying the local flora and fauna, recording his findings in a well documented diary, or looking through his tripod-mounted brass telescope, which had pride of place on the upstairs balcony of his house.

It was this piece of equipment which first drew his attention to a nasty piece of work called Axel Perez. Being a fine morning, the harbour-master had decided to breakfast on his balcony, periodically interrupting his meal to scan the horizon with his treasured telescope. At first he thought nothing of the small dust cloud he had spotted in the distance heading the town's way from the direction of the rope ferry. As he picked up his coffee cup, he had dismissed it as a localized swirl of wind — but as he took a sip, he realized there was no wind: the air was warm and still.

Slapping his coffee cup down on the table, he refocused his telescope. Six riders in no apparent hurry. He adjusted the scope some more and was able to make out some facial detail. These riders looked mean, out to make trouble, and he knew that today, in the little town of Faux-Port, there were too few people to stop them.

★ ★ ★

Axel Perez was feeling good today, and he knew why. Not only did he enjoy this sort of work, but he was getting paid for it, as well. A man of some intellect but little formal education, he had always held a fascination for law and order, how some folk wanted to uphold it and others chose to break it. In fact he had tried being a sheriff himself once, but had found the discipline and dedication required were not to his liking. After all, Axel Perez was a free spirit, and being such had decided to pursue his natural interest in law and order from the other side: the outlaw side.

He had tried robbing banks with a limited degree of success, but based on his experiences, had decided it required too much effort and risk for an uncertain payout. He much preferred receiving a specified sum to lead a small gang to threaten other people against their will, on someone else's behalf. He saw himself as a sort of enforcer of other people's rules and values — which was why he had made his way to the Cove. He thought this kind of work could emanate from such a place, and he had been proved right. With the help of the top man's sidekick, Conway MacPherson, he had chosen a small, select gang of men to carry out the top man's bidding.

★   ★   ★

By the time the harbour-master had taken it on himself to travel to Russen and seek help, it was too late. The Perez gang, who were firmly ensconced in the local saloon, felt irritated that apart from the barman, there was no one around for them to intimidate. Well, that was until Cornelius Fox arrived for his regular mid-morning whiskey.

'An' who might you be, mister?' Axel asked, leaning back against the bar and looking Mr Fox up and down with an air of disdain.

'I, sir, am Cornelius Fox. Editor and proprietor of the local news sheet, at your service. And pray, who might you good gentlemen be?'

'Yer might say that we're political

canvassers,' Perez replied, spitting on the floor for emphasis. 'For the forthcomin' county seat elections. Who might you be votin' for, mister uh, Fox?'

'Ah,' said Cornelius Fox, feeling confident about the chosen topic for conversation. 'I am supporting Russen, as, of course, does my newspaper. Here,' he said, taking a copy out of his leather satchel. 'You can read my reasons, here.' He offered the paper to two of Perez's men who were standing close by. They stared perplexed at the article. It was obvious that they were illiterate. Embarrassed by their ignorance, Axel snatched the paper from them and started to read out loud.

'A vote for Russen in the promised county seat elections is a vote for decency, and law and order. Huh,' Perez grunted. 'It is a cosmop? What's that?'

'Cosmopolitan,' said Cornelius.

'Oh. It is a cosmopolitan town, one of the few that successfully blends legacies of the west and east. In terms of its western influences, Russen has been the pioneering force of this county ever since the cattle drovers first established the town. In terms of its eastern influences, it has brought the culture of good living enjoyed by many on the eastern seaboard to the frontier with its love of food, fine wine and entertainment. As such, it lights a beacon for the whole of the United States as to how communities should live together and work and trade with each other. Indeed, it is this ability to which the people of Faux-Port owe their good fortune. Long may their legacy of being our county seat holder, continue. Vote for Russen!'

Axel Perez let the news sheet fall into a puddle of spilt beer on the bar top. 'Sorry, Cornelius,' he said enjoying the look of alarm on the other man's face. 'But you ain't got this quite right. It's too sentimental, yer see. Folks won't thank yer fer recommendin' they vote on sentimental grounds. They wan' more tangible reasons, like what value to the county does a town bring, which warrants gettin' their vote. Yer see what I mean? Look.' He bade Cornelius sit down and take out his notebook and pencil. 'I'll dictate it to yer.'

Axel took out his gun and tapped the barrel against the side of his head like an educated man might do with a pencil when deep in thought. He then tapped it on the table next to Cornelius's notebook, to signal to the scared editor that he needed to get ready to write.

'My last article recommended votin' for Russen, if yer choosin' to vote on sentimental grounds,' Axel paused. 'Yer got that down, Cornelius?' Cornelius Fox nodded nervously. 'But it has been pointed out to me that people should really be votin' on who deserves to win because of the overall value they bring to the county. Russen is in long term decline. It no longer contributes directly to the wealth of the county. In fact with its collection of the county taxes, it takes away. The people of Faux-Port can't afford to put most of their eggs in this particular rotten basket. Hey, d'yer like that food reference, Cornelius? You had one in your article, I've got one in mine.' Axel laughed at his cleverness.

'Very good, very good,' said Cornelius quickly, anxious for this humiliation to be drawn to a close as soon as possible.

'The people of Faux-Port should be hitchin' their wagons not to a declining source of wealth but to a risin' one, because that's where the future lies. Underground in the mines of Grainger's Cove. So vote for value, vote for increased wealth, vote for Grainger's Cove! What d'yer think, Cornelius? Yer gonna print that in yer next edition?'

'I'll, I'll think about it.' Perez touched the tip of his gun barrel against Cornelius's right temple and pulled back the hammer with his thumb.

'What d'yer jest say?' Perez demanded. He spat on Cornelius's notebook.

'Sorry, I was feelin' confused,' Cornelius said feebly, shaking his head. 'I'll do it. I'll do it!'

'Good,' said Axel, 'I'd hate to come back next week an' find that you hadn't!'

★　★　★

'What's new? Anythin'?' Ervine Fulbeck asked the county records clerk.

'Not a lot,' the clerk replied. 'The harbour-master from Faux-Port's been in. He says he's seen six riders, unsavoury types, makin' their way to town. He knows it's speculation on his part, but he's concerned that they might be about to intimidate the locals as to how they should vote in the county seat elections. He's waitin' in the library for a reply. What should I tell him?'

'Mm, that's interestin',' Ervine said. 'I might need to talk to the state governor about that. Tell the harbour-master we'll send someone such as

Floyd Greenburn as soon as possible, as acting sheriff.'

'OK, Mr Mayor. Oh, an' one other thing,' the clerk said.

'An' what's that?' Ervine enquired.

'I've had a chance to check through the contents of the returned chest,' the clerk said, 'and there's a file missin'.'

'How come?' Ervine said indignantly.

''Fraid I dunno, Mr Mayor,' the clerk replied. 'But it's the Civil War museum file with all the curator's speculations an' his letter to Governor Peters, requestin' research fundin'.'

'Damn!' Ervine exclaimed. 'I will definitely need to talk to the state governor about that!'

⋆   ⋆   ⋆

By the time the harbour-master had returned from his boat trip to Russen, the enchanting sleepy atmosphere of Faux-Port had changed to one of fear and menace. Axel Perez and his gang had taken over the saloon, where they had welcomed nearly two dozen 'immigrants' from other parts of the county who were starting to erect a small tent city by the harbour. The harbourmaster stormed into Cornelius Fox's office demanding an explanation.

'What's been goin' on in my absence, Cornelius? Who are all these strangers? They can't erect their filthy tents all around my harbour! It'll spread disease an' damage our produce!'

'Calm down, calm down, Jim,' said Cornelius. 'We can't do anything about it until help arrives. I'd heard you'd gone to raise the alarm. How did you get on, on that front? Did you speak to Mayor Fulbeck?'

'No, not directly. I dealt through the records clerk, but he told me that Fulbeck would send someone as soon as possible to act as sheriff. Floyd Greenburn or someone like him, Cornelius. The mayor was goin' to get the governor to endorse it, but I was assured it would be a formality.'

'Well, I must say that's a relief,' said

Cornelius. 'Let's hope it is Greenburn. He's a good man. I think he might have his work cut out with this Perez character, but if he needs reinforcements, I am sure he will get them. Meantime, we've all got to try and stay calm and avoid upsetting this hot head, as best as we can. Oh, no!' he groaned. 'It looks like Perez is heading this way.' Cornelius's office door flew open, in response to the hard kick from the sole of Perez's left boot.

'See yer got a visitor, Cornelius,' Perez said, as he chewed on a plug of tobacco.

'Oh, this is Jim the harbour-master,' Cornelius said, introducing his visitor. 'Jim, this is Axel Perez. He is canvassing on behalf of the Cove and seeking the support of the people of Faux-Port in the county seat election.'

'Who are these people erecting tents by my harbour? Are they anythin' to do with you, Mister Perez?' Jim enquired in a matter-of-fact way. 'Cos they can't stay there, yer know. They're stoppin' the smooth runnin' of the harbour.'

'Well, these poor souls gotta go somewhere, Jim, an' the hotel's already full. Maybe some of 'em can stay in your nice white house, over there,' said Axel pointing at Jim's home. 'D'yer wan' me to ask 'em to move in with yer?'

'No!' replied Jim sharply. 'Who are they, anyway?'

'Who are they? They're what yer call immigrants, lookin' fer somewhere new to live. They don't wanna be pushed around the county. They wan' somewhere they can put down roots. Where they can register to vote for the Cove.'

'I know you're tryin' to intimidate the people of Faux-Port.'

'I am not tryin' to intimidate anyone,' Axel Perez interjected sharply. 'I am trying to appeal to people's sense of reason.'

'OK, OK You're trying to influence people, but it's not practical to bring in extra people. We just don't have the facilities to accommodate large groups of men in this town.'

'You're so damned right, Cornelius,' Axel said sarcastically. 'An' that's what I came to see yer about. I wan' yer to print some hand bills an' post 'em all over town. All they need to say is this: Sporting Ladies Urgently Required to Welcome New Residents. Womenfolk who are already resident of this town will be ineligible for selection to these positions, provided they and their men folk vote now for Grainger's Cove in the forthcoming county seat elections. Ballot papers are available from Cornelius Fox's office!'

* * *

'Sorry to call you in early evenin', Bill. It's about two matters that I need to bring you up to speed with. I'll be as quick as I can as yer probably wantin' to get back before nightfall.'

'Don't worry, I'll probably stay over. What's botherin' you, Ervine?'

'The first one concerns some potential intimidation of voters at Faux-Port.'

'We're not doin' that, are we? I don't want Russen intimidating voters. That'll be the end of any chance of winning.'

'No, no, I agree. I suspect it's the Cove. But if it is goin' on, and hopefully it is, it could be to our advantage.' William Peters gave Ervine a strange look. 'Well, if it can be proved that there is intimidation goin' on and we happened to lose the election because of it, the courts would undoubtedly declare the result of the election null and void.'

'That's good thinking, Ervine,' William said. 'And how would you prove it?'

'I was gonna ask Floyd Greenburn to investigate. A job right up his street. I've made arrangements to meet him mid mornin', tomorrow in my office.'

'Good,' William said. 'And what's the other issue?' Ervine explained about the missing file. The whole chest problem was becoming messier and messier, but Ervine was not surprised. It was typical of most of his dealings with William Peters.

'So, whoever put the chest back wanted that file, by the looks of things,' William said thoughtfully. 'Our main suspect for retrieving the chest was Floyd Greenburn. That's what your predecessor asked him to do, but he's never claimed responsibility for doing it. Besides, what would he want with that museum file?'

'Dunno, Bill, I dunno. Do you still want him to investigate the intimidation rumours?' Ervine asked.

'Of course, he'll be good at that. It may be we jest need to keep a closer eye on him, and as he will be working for us on the investigation, it gives us a good opportunity to do that.'

11

Floyd rolled himself a smoke and sat down on a wooden barrel on the edge of the quayside while awaiting the return of the rope ferry. His horse stood quietly by his side. He had accepted Fulbeck's proposal to temporarily act as sheriff of Faux-Port. The situation didn't really surprise him; circumstances in Holmbury County made it ripe for a county seat war. It certainly wouldn't be the first county to experience such shenanigans, and it probably wouldn't be the last.

The key was to maintain order and prevent descent into violence, kidnap and murder, which had characterized other county seat wars. The ferryman had warned Floyd that earlier on, he had had a number of groups of men whom he described as drunken rabble rousers, men from the Cove heading for

Faux-Port. Rather than ride in alone to Faux-Port, Floyd had already decided that once on the west bank, he would first ride north to Denton and pick up Chancy and Russ. As he raised his smoke to his mouth, he felt a gentle light touch on his elbow. It was Sarah Tamswaite.

'I am sorry to disengage you from your thoughts,' she said apologetically, 'but I would be very much obliged if we could have a brief, quiet conversation.'

'That's OK, Miss Tamswaite,' said Floyd, slightly surprised. 'What would you like to say?'

'You may think this very presumptuous of me, but I just wanted to warn you to be careful. In my line of work, I have contact with all sorts of different people who know all sorts of other people. So I know, for example, that William Peters is aware that not all the files in the county records chest were returned with the chest. Underneath his public exterior, Mr Peters is a paranoid man. He thinks that someone is after him. Paranoid people can be dangerous people.'

'But what's that got to do with me?' Floyd asked, his curiosity aroused. 'Why are you tellin' me this?'

'Because,' Sarah hesitated and took a deep breath. 'Because I recognized you as one of the three men who returned the missing chest to the back steps of the town hall. It was after midnight, and all three of you wore masks but I recognized you from your build and your gait.' She stared him straight in the eye. Before he could speak, she carried on. 'I am sorry,' she said, 'but I don't expect you to admit it, and yet I don't expect you to deny it either. I could see you quite clearly from my bedroom window.'

'So, so what do you wan' from me?' Floyd asked, feeling a little speechless.

'I don't want anything from you, Mr Greenburn, other than that you promise to look after yourself. And you have my word that I have not mentioned my midnight sighting of you to anyone, and neither will I. Only you and I know about it. Like I say, my work at the Temperance Society exposes me, more than most, to various people's addictions and bad habits, so I know how to keep confidences.'

'I can't help but worry that that may make you vulnerable and put your own well-being at risk,' said Floyd partially thinking of the gin he had smelt on her breath when they had met earlier, and partially of her stress from having to live with the bottled-up knowledge of other people's dirty secrets. 'I thank you for your honesty and trust, sincerely I do,' he said, expressing his admiration for her courage. 'I will heed your warning.'

'Thank you,' Sarah said, looking a little coy. 'You must understand that I am sharing this with you and you only, because I sense that you are basically a good man who cares about the common people. Unfortunately there are not many like you in this county. You must trust me when I tell you that many of those in positions of influence are not good men. They are bad men, just out for their own ends.'

12

'How many of them are there supposed to be, Michel?' Kittie Rousseau asked her husband.

'About twenty of 'em, apparently,' her husband replied. 'Takin' their orders from some hired thug by the name of Axel Perez,' he added, putting on his gun belt.

'It's years since you wore that gun,' Kittie pointed out. 'Be careful, Michel. There's no need to be brave. Life is more important.'

'I know,' Michel agreed. 'It is a long time since I've had to fire a gun in anger. I can't afford to make a mistake, if I have to use it. I'm gonna go now. Wish me luck.'

'May God be with you, husband,' Kittie said, with a slight tremor in her voice. 'We'll be following on, not far behind you in the wagon.' She turned to her sixteen-year-old son as her husband left the farm house. 'Here, Jean. Take this.' She handed the young man the 'yellow boy' '66 Winchester, her husband's first ever rifle. The boy loved rabbit stew and consequently was very familiar with how to use it as a hunting weapon.

Taking hold of the gun gave Jean confidence. He had never seen his parents like this before, in a state of trepidation, with his father having to ride into town armed. He wished he had gone with his father to protect him, albeit that Michel was certainly the better shot out of the two of them. Then again, he needed to protect his mother. There were rumours starting to circulate that it wasn't safe to leave your womenfolk alone at home, and there was no way that he would be able to persuade his mother to stay at home with his father's life potentially under threat.

★   ★   ★

As the Rousseau wagon reached Main Street, Kittie and Jean witnessed a commotion outside the saloon. A group of men, strangers from outside Faux-Port, had formed the obligatory, jeering circle around their source of entertainment. Kittie stopped the wagon someway short of the saloon, but from their seat above the horse, they had a grandstand view. Axel Perez had his arm around the waist of one of the Rousseaus' neighbours, while the woman's brother was desperately trying to attack him. But every time the brother made a lunge, Perez lifted the woman off the ground and swung her round in front of her brother, so that she kicked him with her flailing legs and the brother had to reduce his momentum to avoid hitting her.

'Let go of me, you! You vicious beast!' the woman screamed.

'All you need to do is fill in the ballot paper to vote for the Cove an' I'll let you go, little darlin',' Perez said with a sneer.

'You'll never force the people of Faux-Port to act against their will!' the woman shouted out. Perez paid her last protest no attention. He had seen a man who had worked his way to the front of the crowd, go for his gun. It was Michel Rousseau. Perez dropped the woman on the ground drew his gun and fired. The bullet winged Michel's wrist. He dropped his pistol on the floor. Axel Perez slowly walked over to Michel and smashed him hard across the face with the back of his hand. Michel fell to the floor. The crowd widened their circle to make this new piece of entertainment centre stage.

★　★　★

Their journey south along the Denton Trail almost complete, Floyd, Russ and Chancy reached the outskirts of Faux-Port harbour. They slowly picked their way through the small tent city that had sprung up overnight, surprised to find it empty.

'Is this jest a bit of posturin'?' Chancy asked. 'There's no one about.'

'I think they might all be in Main Street,' said Russ. 'Sounds like there might be a raucous crowd up there, listen.' They stopped their horses.

'The pattern of that noise, sounds like some poor soul might be takin' a beatin',' Chancy added.

'Let's walk the horses to the back door of the hotel an' take a look,' Floyd suggested.

★   ★   ★

'Sheriff Greenburn,' the hotelier greeted Floyd as he walked up to the counter. 'Boy, are we glad to see you! We've got trouble here, big time. Michel Rousseau is takin' a beatin' from Axel Perez. It's stirred up the crowd. It could all get out of hand if they're lookin' fer blood!'

'Can we get up on the roof?' Floyd asked.

'Yep. Let me get the ladder an' the key,' the hotelier replied.

'Shoot him, son. Shoot him now, while he's got his back to us.' Jean rested the butt of the rifle against his shoulder and lowered and raised the lever action ready to fire. 'Go on, now,' Kittie urged.

'I can't do it, Ma,' Jean told her. 'When Pa taught me how to handle a gun, he stressed that you never, ever shoot a man in the back.'

'That's cos your father's a good man.' Axel instinctively started to turn around, and catching the glint of sunlight reflecting off the rifle's brass receiver, out of the corner of his eye, he turned to face Jean.

'Go fer it, kid,' he said. 'I'll give yer a chance.' Jean pulled the trigger. The bullet whistled over Axel's head. 'As I thought, a 'yellow boy' rifle for a yeller kid!' Quick as a flash, Perez's gun was out of its holster and trained on Jean and his mother. 'Better not touch that lever action agen, boy,' he warned menacingly. 'Now, git down both of yer, off of that wagon.' The boy got down first, followed by his mother. He dropped the rifle on the ground.

'OK. Torch the wagon!' Perez ordered two of his men.

★   ★   ★

'Why did he shoot over Perez's head?' Chancy asked as they peered over the edge of the roof edge and through the smoke of the burning wagon. 'That ain't like a country boy.'

'Country boys may be deadly accurate at shootin' rabbits and wild boar,' said Floyd, 'but they ain't no good at shootin' humans, especially when they have to look 'em in the eye. Experienced it meself when I was a bit older than that kid. An' it was rife in the Civil War. For the amount of ammunition used there should have been a lot more deaths, but many folk would shoot over the enemy's heads cos they couldn't bear to kill another human bein'. An' these folks are gentle people — market gardeners, not even soldiers, let alone gun slingers. Can either of you boys see a clear shot on Perez?' Russ and Chancy both signalled negative. 'We'll have to wait until this smoke clears a bit.'

★ ★ ★

'Get down there on the ground with yer pa, boy!' Perez barked. 'Now, Mrs Rousseau. Yer a mighty fine-lookin' woman, yer know,' he said leeringly. 'An' yer got no way of gettin' home tonight now, since yer made me burn yer wagon. Perhaps you'd like to stay with me tonight?' The crowd started to snigger. 'I don't think yer gonna be a widow for long, somehow! Jed, Pete!' Two of the younger members of his crew stepped forward. 'Go find the preacher. Tell him to prepare for two funerals and a wedding!'

★ ★ ★

'C'mon, move this way a bit more,' Floyd whispered quietly. 'There's a gap in the smoke.' He watched from his roof-top hideout as Perez drew his pistol and pulled back the hammer.

'Hold the woman steady!' Perez shouted to his men. The outlaw moved round the two bodies on the ground deciding whether to kill Jean or Michel first.

'Go for Michel, first.' Floyd whispered hoping to save the boy. But Perez thought he'd spare the kid from watching his father die first and from the agony of waiting to be next. Unbeknown to him he stepped into a clearing in the smoke. Floyd pulled the trigger and Axel Perez dropped his gun as the bullet tore into his hand. Chancy and Russ opened up with their six-guns, spraying the ground around Axel's feet with bullets. Michel picked Axel's gun up off the ground and joined in. Perez was forced to bullet dance, much to the crowd's amusement. They no longer laughed with him, but at him. Floyd signalled for the shooting to stop.

'Take yer boots off, Perez!' he shouted down from the hotel roof top, 'an' throw 'em on the fire!' The crowd laughed louder as the egotistical outlaw was forced to undergo a ritual of humiliation similar to the one he had been imposing on others.

'An' now the rest of you strangers in town, do the same!' The crowd fell silent. Floyd fired his gun in the air. 'Get on with it!' he shouted. Slowly the men did as they were ordered. Walking in stockinged feet can hurt, but not as much as taking a bullet through the foot.

⋆　⋆　⋆

It was a strange yet sobering sight to watch a line of nearly thirty men walking in single file the few miles to the Russen rope ferry with only socks on their feet. Even the strongest and toughest looking were reduced to hobbling wrecks, slowly and carefully picking their way, a step at a time, over the stony ground, completely at the mercy of any predator. Floyd, Russ and Chancy stayed with them until they were over half way to the ferry and had become more interested in keeping going than turning back.

'That was funny, but kinda cruel,' Chancy remarked as they wheeled their horses round to head back to Denton.

'Yep, but we achieved what we wan'ed without a blood bath, an' that's the main thing,' said Floyd. 'They'll be very few of 'em who'll wanna try that agen.'

'An' that includes Perez. He's all washed up round these parts now. His credibility's all shot to pieces!' They laughed at Russ's joke before falling silent for a while.

'Did anyone see that Jed an' Pete?' Chancy asked, breaking the silence. 'I don't recall seein' 'em in the line of bootless warriors, an' we rode up an' down that a few times.'

'Maybe, they're still in Faux-Port?' Russ suggested.

'I reckon' they hot footed it out of there when all the shootin' started,' Floyd said. 'They've either headed west or gone up to Denton to try and sneak a boat ride across the river to the Cove.'

'Hope they're not gonna create any trouble up there,' said Chancy.

'I don't think they'd survive long, especially if they tried to sleep rough. Them against a wild cat, I'd back the animal every time,' said Floyd. 'It's Marlin Bart we need to be concerned about. We've foiled his little scheme fer now an' he's gonna be a bit mad. The one thing we can count on is that he won't give up, so we need to consider what his next move might be, an' stay one step ahead.'

13

'I'm afraid I won't be stoppin' after this evening's meeting,' William Peters said, referring to the regular weekly get-together of the Holmbury County Temperance Society.

'Oh,' Sarah replied quietly. She reached for the gin bottle, discreetly placed in the small bookcase by the side of her bed — a small act of celebration, although the state governor automatically assumed it was an act of disappointment. 'I see,' she said.

'I have to be home tonight.'

'How is your wife?' Sarah enquired politely, pouring herself a tot.

'She's very poorly. The doctor doesn't think that she has long to go.' He paused. 'I thought you'd stopped drinking that stuff. I thought we'd agreed. That's a fighting man's drink, as you should well know. It's certainly not a lady's drink, feisty as you can be at times. It can attract the wrong kind of male attention.' She parried the slight insult by initially saying nothing, and then, after taking a sip, displayed a brief period of calm delight.

'I had stopped,' Sarah replied, 'but I've run out of laudanum.'

'I know it's hard for you, Sarah, living your life as a secret, and that will all change soon,' the state governor said, 'but you have to understand that, in my position, it is embarrassing for me. Nobody has said anything, not that they would, but as executive trustee of this Temperance Society, I can't afford to have its sole executive director, incidentally appointed by me, reeking of gin!'

'But you don't mind me drinking laudanum?' Sarah said curtly, seeking confirmation of the earlier conversation to which he referred. 'Not only does it contain alcohol but it is alcohol mixed with opiates!'

'Of course I don't mind,' William

confirmed, putting his arm around her waist. 'As long as you don't drink too much of it. Laudanum is a respectable drink for middle class women. Indeed, in moderation it has health benefits for women. It helps with — well, female problems. No one is goin' to think the worse of you for taking that. Many women supporters of temperance are habitual users of opium. You aren't suffering from flushes or any other side effects, are you?'

'No, Billy,' she replied. Her use of his nickname they both regarded as an unwritten term of endearment. But for her, on this occasion, it was a manipulative term, one which not only enabled her to subtly remove his arm from her waist, but also to change the subject. 'Tell me more about the condition of your poor, dear, dear wife.'

'Like I say,' said William, 'the doctor believes she has not long to go. Her ailment has all the symptoms of being a terminal condition, and to ease the pain he is regularly increasing the doses of morphine. She surely can't be long for this world. But then, after a respectable grieving period, you and I can go public about our relationship and marry.' Sarah took another sip of her gin. 'Sarah Tamswaite,' the state governor continued, 'I know you well enough to know that you were not brought up to be just another middle-class woman. You were not even brought up to be a state governor's wife. You were brought up to be the wife of a United States president. President Peters to be precise!' William poured himself a glass of the gin. 'Here's to President Peters and the first lady of the United States of America, Sarah Peters!' he said, clinking his glass against hers.

★   ★   ★

Like a true lush, Sarah sat on her bed and took the last swig of gin that she had in her apartment, directly from the bottle. She had made it through the meeting, her reputation among the good and the great of the Temperance Movement unsullied. They would have been shocked to see such behaviour and attitude. But that was her skill — a smooth operator in the public arena. William had left straight after the meeting as he had promised. Consequently, she was surprised to hear the knock on the door downstairs. Had William forgotten something or changed his mind and decided to stay after all? Or was it perhaps Floyd Greenburn wanting to pursue their earlier conversation? She ran downstairs, her heart in her mouth and opened the door.

'Ah, Mr Chi Ling. It's you,' she said trying to quell any note of surprise there may have been in her voice.

'Missy Sarah,' Mr Chi Ling said. 'Here is your weekly order of cleaned garments and linens.' He handed her two large parcels wrapped in brown paper and tied with string.

'I take those away?' he enquired

pointing to the laundry basket, just inside the door.

'Yes, please,' Sarah replied.

'I'll put them on the wagon,' he said, picking up the laundry basket, 'and fetch you your weekly supply of laudanum. Is there anything else I can do for you, missy Sarah?'

'Yes, please, Mr Ling. I want you to double my weekly supply of laudanum.'

14

Floyd had two offices on the site of his lumber works. One was down the bottom of the mountainside, next to the sawmill and adjacent to his small ranch with its riverside views. The other, the smaller of the two, was half way up the mountain next to the top of the log flume. When the men weren't cutting down trees in the surrounding area, he often used the latter office as a retreat, for when he needed to reflect and plan.

Now was such an occasion. He had taken out Adison Marson's file again and reread the old man's request to State Governor Peters, seeking funding to visit the grave of Captain Ransom Travis — Travis, the man who had sent Floyd's cousin to visit the hangman's noose, twenty-six years ago, for a crime he didn't commit. With evidence verified on the say-so of just one man,

Captain Emmett Aldstone. Both captains then appeared to have mysteriously gone missing, but now, the fate of one of them could possibly be put beyond doubt. Marson's application for funding was innocuous: just a reasonable request to verify if someone else's supposition was true, and if so, add a sentence of closure for one of the captains at least, to the history books. He checked the date on Adison's letter: it was exactly two weeks before the day he died. Surely the governor could have replied in that time.

For a brief moment Floyd felt like confronting Peters himself, but realized that he would have to lie pretty convincingly about how he had found out about Marson's letter. Besides, there was probably a good reason why Peters hadn't replied — for example, the request may have been deprioritized by the records clerk. On the other hand, why hadn't the governor actioned the request anyway, after Adison Marson's death? The public would surely welcome having the record put straight. It would have been another quick win for the newly appointed William Peter's credibility, to demonstrate that he saw this particular matter of historical importance no less a priority than he saw the county seat election as one of current importance. Yet Sarah had warned Floyd that William Peters was a paranoid man and thought somebody was after him, strange as that may seem. She clearly knew more than she was letting on, but understandably didn't want to put her own safety at risk. There was only one way out of this dilemma, Floyd decided, and that was to visit Honer County and find Travis's grave himself.

'Floyd, Floyd!' It was Chancy.

'In the office!' Floyd replied. Having made his decision, he locked the Adison Marson file away in his safe, his mind back in the current moment. 'What's up, Chancy?'

'We think those two varmints who Perez sent to get the preacher, have been hidin' out half way up the mountainside. Russ found the remains of a camp fire which is still warm, not that far down from here, on the other side of the flume. I found some hoof marks, suggestin' two horses!' Floyd looked at his watch.

'Go down to the sawmill and tell the foreman to delay sendin' the first loggin' party of the day up here, until further notice. Also, tell him to switch the flume away from the sawmill into the overflow escape channel. An' Chancy, fire two bullets in the air to let me know when he's done all that.'

'OK, boss,' said Chancy mounting his horse. By the time Chancy fired the signal, Russ had joined Floyd. As the echo of Chancy's second bullet faded away, Floyd and Russ saw movement much lower down the mountainside.

'D'yer see that?' Floyd asked. 'South-east of the sawmill?' Russ raised the telescope to his eye. 'Yeah, it's them all right. Jed an' Pete, the dynamic duo. They're on foot, cautiously leadin' their horses towards the escape flume. Chancy's gunfire must have spooked 'em a bit! Yer gonna ride the flume?'

'Why not? I've got some plans for those boys. Help me lift the dugout.' The two men lifted the large log, which had been hollowed out into a canoe, from its storage place underneath the flume and tied it in position on top. Floyd climbed up the framework and into the craft. 'Cut the rope, Russ!' he screamed. 'Here we go!'

He wedged himself down low in the boat, his shoulders up against the back, and his knees bent with the soles of his feet pushed hard against the front bulwark. He grabbed hold of the rope as the front of the boat moved forwards into space, as if it thought it was a bird that could fly. At the equilibrium point, gravity played its heavy hand and the front of the boat lurched forwards and downwards, crashing into the trough of water beneath it. The dugout quickly picked up speed as it descended the first gradient, briefly riding up the side wall as it rounded the first bend. It gained more momentum as it descended the second gradient, reaching galloping speed within seconds — but unlike a horseman, allowing the rider no control whatsoever!

As it reached the bottom of the gradient, the flume flattened out and Floyd felt the boat slow down, eventually coming to a stop, the final slight increase in gradient acting as a brake. To reduce the chances of being seen, he lay down flat in the boat as best as he could and listened to the surrounding environment. All he could hear was the sound of the wind gently blowing in the trees, the occasional birdsong, and the sound of the water settling in the trough of the log flume. He sat up, looked around quickly, and climbed out of the boat. If he and Russ had calculated correctly, Jed and Pete should be walking towards him rather than away from him. He perched himself behind a rock on the side of the trail and just waited and listened.

'Did yer hear that, Jed? Sounded like rushin' water, but now it's stopped.'

'Yeah, it's the log flume,' Pete replied nonchalantly. He regarded himself as the smarter of the two of them. 'A log has just come down.'

'But why send one log down on its own an' not loads more, one after the other?' Jed challenged without understanding the potential significance of his question.

'Probably the last one got stuck. They do that, yer know. Probably been up there hours an' jest managed to free itself.'

'Oh, I never knew that happened.'

'Naw, you wouldn't have,' Pete said slightly irritated at the naivety of his new 'pardner'. 'Jest concentrate on listenin' an' lookin' to see if there's anyone trackin' us. We don't need to discuss every noise or movement.'

They rode in silence, at a walking pace for the next minute or so. Jed then wondered if he had heard the sound of a six-shooter hammer being pulled back: that ominous double click, the first click a different pitch from the second, as the chamber made its brief clockwise journey to align the next bullet. But he decided not to mention it. Lots of noises sounded similar, and he didn't want to upset Pete again by sounding even more stupid than he felt he had, the last time he opened his mouth. Taking everything into account, he thought he had found a 'good'un' in Pete, someone worth keeping on side.

'Goin' somewhere, boys?' They both span round in their saddles, only to find themselves staring down the barrel of Floyd's six-shooter.

★　★　★

'Where's this work yer wan' done, mister?' Pete asked. 'Where yer takin' us?'

'Deep into Honer County,' Floyd replied.

'You said you'd pay us, mister? How much?' Jed asked. 'We've been travellin' a few hours already, an' as far as I'm concerned that's all workin' time.'

'You drive a hard bargain, don't yer, Jed?' Floyd commented.

'Yer said it was important work, mister, an' we're skilled labour,' Pete added, getting in on the act.

'How much did that critter, Perez, pay yer?'

'A dollar a day or any part thereof,' said Pete remembering the specific wording of the deal that the big Cornish man, Conway MacPherson, had struck with them.

'Well, seein' as my job's so important an' you boys are so skilled, I'll double yer rate. Two dollars each. If yer good workers, it won't take yer a day.' Both men tried to hide displaying a sudden feeling of self-importance.

'When do we get our guns back, mister?' Jed asked.

'Don't push yer luck, Jed,' Pete whispered to his colleague.

'No, don't push yer luck, Jed,' Floyd repeated. 'You'll get 'em back when I say you've finished yer work.'

★ ★ ★

It was dark by the time they reached the cemetery, but fortunately there was a full moon that night, which cast an eerie pale glow over many of the tombstones.

'Now,' Floyd said, 'Can either of yer read?' Jed nodded his head, but it was obvious from Pete's complete lack of bodily movement or facial expression that he was illiterate. 'OK, Jed, I wan' you to walk around the tombstones and look for one with the name Travis on it.'

'But there's loads of 'em, ain't anyone gonna help me?'

'No. I'm gonna sit down an' have a smoke an' brew me some coffee. I ain't so 'hands-on' as yer last boss, Perez. But then agen, I'm payin' yer double. Take your mate, Pete, with yer. Pete, watch an' learn.'

174

It took the two press-ganged men fifteen minutes to find a grave with the name Travis enscribed on the tomb-stone. Excited, Jed called Floyd over. It was the one he had hoped to find. The simple tombstone read:

Here lies our beloved son
Ransom Travis
Died 4th January 1865
Age 34

The grave, which appeared to be reasonably well maintained, lay next to an almost identical one with a similar inscription, but the name had been largely but crudely erased, probably by a piece of rock. The legible part of the inscription read:

Here lies our dutiful son

Died 17th July 1870
Age 39

'Can we take a smoke break now,

mister?' Pete called out.

'Yeah, an' is there any coffee goin'?' Jed asked.

'You got any mugs?' Floyd enquired.

'Naw, mister.'

'Well, yer ain't got anythin' to drink it out of then,' said Floyd. 'Five minutes' smoke break, then.'

Seems like Ransom may have had a brother, Floyd thought to himself, not having heard any mention of it before. He wondered why someone had tried to desecrate the brother's grave. He ran his hand over the scratched stone. It was possible in the moonlight to still see the remnants of an inscription where the stone mason's chisel had penetrated the stone more deeply and precisely than the rough edge of whatever scratching implement had been used. He picked up some dry dirt, spat on it, and rubbed it across the area where the deceased's name once stood. The damp earth started to wedge in what remained of the chiselled crevices, suggesting what looked like letter formations.

Floyd sat on his haunches and stared at the result of his handy work. He wondered if he could work out what the actual letters were supposed to be. The hardest part was deciphering the first letter of the inscription. He mentally started working his way through the alphabet, and as he got beyond half way, began to think that this was perhaps a bad idea. But that was until he tried the letter *W*, which appeared to fit. The proof would be if he could find the second letter, which turned out to be an *I*. Within ten minutes he realized that the name that had once graced the now desecrated tombstone was *WILL-IAM PETERS*.

'You done with us now, mister?' Pete called out. 'Can we have our money?'

'Nope. I need you boys to dig up the two graves. I wanna see what's inside.'

'What we gonna dig with, mister?'

'Your hands, if need be. Look over there, there's a half-dug grave. They may have left some spades there, or planks of wood.' Pete skulked over to take a look.

'It's your lucky day, mister!' he called back. 'I've found three spades!' He came back with them and offered one to Floyd. 'Many hands make light work, eh?' Floyd let the spade drop to the ground.

'I don't wanna hold you skilled workers up,' said Floyd. 'Remember, that's why I'm payin' yer good money. To get on with it. Besides, it's time for my smoke break.'

★ ★ ★

It took Jed and Pete a good hour to clear the soil from the top of each coffin. They called Floyd over to take a look at their handiwork. He made them wipe the mud off the brass plaques that decorated each of the coffins. One bore the name Ransom Travis, and the other, as he had expected, William Peters.

'Open 'em both up!' he ordered, as

he sat down on a nearby grave with his legs astride, his knees in the air and his back leaning up against the tombstone. He put his gun down between his thighs and covered it with his hat. Pete was working on Ransom's coffin and had managed to partially remove the lid when Jed called Pete for help. He was struggling, but with the leverage of an extra spade widening the gap between the casket and its lid, it became easier to open the coffin up. They stared in shock at the perfectly formed skeleton that lay before them. There wasn't a blemish, no broken bones, no bullet marks.

'Couldn't have had many enemies, this one,' Jed whispered.

'What's this?' said Pete, bending down and picking up a small parcel of oilcloth which had been laid next to the skeleton. From its weight and shape there was clearly something wrapped inside. He carefully removed the oil cloth to reveal an old Smith & Wesson Model 3 revolver.

'Wonder if it still works,' Jed whispered.

'Should do. Looks plenty clean, with metal cartridges an' all. We'll soon see.' Pete climbed back into Travis's grave.

'You boys gone all quiet on me,' said Floyd. 'What gives?'

'Nothin', mister.' Pete said. 'Jest enjoyin' the silence of the night. Listen to how quiet it is, mister.' He teasingly pulled back the hammer of the Model 3 and raised its barrel above the parapet of the grave.

'Yer gonna shoot me, Pete?' Floyd said.

'Afraid so, mister. Take all yer money an' yer horse as well,' said Pete, accidentally knocking the lid off the coffin, as he climbed back out of the grave.

'One last wish, Pete?'

'If yer want, mister. Wouldn't wanna deny yer that. What is it?'

'I swore that when it came to dyin' I always wanned to die with mer hat on mer head.'

'Well, stick it on then, mister.'

'Thanks, Pete.' The lifting of the hat, the revelation of the gun underneath it, and the pulling of the trigger were all too quick for Pete. He took the bullet clean through the heart and fell backwards into the open coffin. Floyd was on his feet in an instant and over to the grave. He looked down at the damaged casket and saw all he needed to see. Pete was dead, and his body was the only one in the coffin.

'That was mean, mister,' Jed said starting to pee himself, frightened that it was his turn next. 'He was unarmed.'

'No, he wasn't. He had a gun.'

'But it probably didn't work. It's probably been lyin' in that grave fer years.' Floyd went over and took the gun from Pete's hand. He fired off two shots, threw the gun back into the coffin, and replaced the lid to make his point.

'He was the brains of our outfit, Pete was, mister.'

'Not from what I saw,' Floyd replied.

'Yer under-sellin' yerself, son.'

'D'yer think so, mister?'

'Well, you're the one still alive, out the two of yer, ain't yer? Suspect yer fell in with the wrong kind of company, son. Look, here's what I'll do fer yer. I'm gonna sit here an' watch yer fill in these two graves, an' make 'em look proper agen. Then I'm gonna let you go. I'll give you yer two dollars, but for good measure I'm gonna give yer Pete's as well. Sure ain't no use to him. But then, I don't wan' yer to darken my door, ever agen.'

'Gee thanks, mister,' said Jed feeling pleased with all the recognition.

★　★　★

As the dawn rose, Floyd decided to take a slight detour on his way back to Denton and visit the site where the Confederate Army had massacred an entire village in 1861. Although he knew where it was, he had never been able to bring himself to visit the site of such wanton brutality that eventually led to the death of his cousin, an innocent man. His venture of the last evening had proved a revelation. It clearly implied that Ransom Travis's death had not only been faked, but even worse, suggested that Travis may have taken on the identity of a dead brother or half-brother, William Peters. It made him feel optimistic. Something inside was telling him that now was the right time to visit the scene of the Honer County civil war atrocity.

It was years since he had travelled this way, and he had forgotten how flat this part of the county was, and how heavily wooded, as well. Paths and trails zigzagged across each other, making it easy for the unsuspecting traveller to get lost. But as the early morning sun rose, its bright light filtering through the trees provided a welcome navigation aid. He kept to the main trail moving north, his horse moving at just walking pace, so he could absorb the geography of the area. Eventually, the trail ran alongside a small but fast-flowing stream, and he knew from what others had told him in the past that he was on the right track.

He soon arrived at a clearing and realized that this was where the village had been, and where the massacre had taken place. There were no visible signs that anything had happened — no plaques, no remains of partially destroyed buildings. Every tell-tale sign had been removed to appease the collective conscience. All that was left was a clearing in a wood with a stream running through it. He rode round the perimeter of the site, noting how tall the trees were and how thick the forest was. This was ancient forest, so it must have been like this long before white settlers discovered the area. The only change the settlers must have made to the environment was to create the clearing to give them easy access to the stream, and to provide flat land on which to build a homestead, plant a few crops, and provide some grazing land for their sheep and goats.

But the one thing that really struck him was how could Captain Emmett Aldstone have testified that although he arrived on the scene fifteen minutes after the slaughter had stopped, he had seen it from afar while approaching the site? The geography of the location ruled that out as a physical possibility. Of course, he could have watched the massacre from the cover of the perimeter woodland, but in that case why hadn't he stepped forward and attempted to stop it?

Floyd thought that this all smacked of a military cover-up to protect the generals and officers, those at the top, from being held accountable. But for him personally, fate had been kind over the last few days and had dealt him a number of new cards, and high value cards at that. All he needed to do now was to work out how best to play them.

15

In the same way that Sarah sensed that he was in danger, Floyd increasingly felt that she was as well. He decided that he had to go and see her and lay his cards directly on the table, including about the smell of alcohol on her breath, and the evidence he had seen implying that a man was living with her, and the sighting of Peters leaving her house.

She looked at him somewhat astounded by his observations, that he could be so bold as to sit in her parlour and virtually accuse her of things, which if forced to, she could explain away. And to think that she had tried to help him by sharing confidences that could put her life in danger. She reached for her bottle of laudanum, but when she came to pour the contents into her glass, she was greeted by just a few drops. She tutted, got up from the table brusquely, and took a small bottle of gin from the cupboard. She walked back into the parlour, sat down and half-filled her glass.

'Look, Sarah, these things that I've just told you, I've only mentioned because I'm concerned about your welfare,' Floyd explained. 'I'm sorry. Maybe I've done this the wrong way around. Maybe I should have told you first what I am going to tell you now. Please hear me out and then, if you want to tell me to mind my own business and to leave, I will do so.' He noticed the look of anger subside from her face. She took a sip of gin, which he hesitantly read as a signal to carry on.

'It's OK,' she said gently. 'I'm sorry as well. Do go on.'

'If you don't already know this, it may shock you.' She looked at him impassively. 'I found out in the small hours of this morning that William Peters appears not to be who he claims to be. I am sorry to be so abrupt, but unfortunately there is much more, which you may, or may not want to hear, depending on your relationship with the man.' He stopped as a lone tear drop fell down her cheek. She remained silent while regaining her composure.

'I feel I can trust you, Floyd, in fact I feel we can trust each other,' Sarah said quietly. 'I definitely want to listen to you but before you continue, I am going to tell you why. Some of what I want to say may shock you too, but we have both gone too far with our warnings. We can't go back now, it's too late for that. We can only go forward by sharing what we know more fully, which in my case means exposing some of the skeletons in my closet. It may help you put what you want to tell me, into context beforehand.'

'May I?' said Floyd reaching for the gin bottle himself.

'Of course,' Sarah said and went and fetched an empty glass. She placed it on the table and then took a deep breath.

'First of all, I am William Peters' mistress. A situation forced on me, not out of choice I emphasize, but out of necessity. Let me explain. Many of the facts relating to the Honer County atrocity of '61 were either played down or denied, and erased from the account. One fact that was not denied but which was certainly played down, of which you may be aware, is that there was a survivor. A five-year-old girl, hidden in a cellar by her mother so that she didn't see the murder of her friends, family and neighbours, and would hopefully survive. Well, that little girl did. It was me.'

Floyd gently touched Sarah's forearm which was resting on the table, to show his compassion. She registered acknowledgement with her eyes, anxious to continue and experience the catharsis of sharing her story.

'Captain Ransom Travis's parents, I suppose out of social conscience, took me in. They were a wealthy aristocratic family of southern stock. They raised me — or more specifically, one of their elderly black maids did, who effectively became my guardian. She and I had much in common, both having been through not dissimilar emotional experiences. The Travises were basically decent people, and very generous with it. In fact, when I was in their care, I had a far better quality of life than I would have done, had I been brought up by my blood family. All the time I was with them however, I never saw or met Ransom Travis. In fact, I don't recall his name ever being mentioned, at least not in my presence.

'I adopted my grandmother's maiden name of Tamswaite to completely divorce myself from being a victim of the atrocity. One way or another, I guess no one completely escapes the ravages of war, and by 1870, Ransom's parents seemed to have prematurely aged and were beginning to suffer ill health. They were unable to maintain their large plantation without slaves, so sold up and moved into a much smaller retirement home, which enabled them at least to continue to enjoy the finer points of the lifestyle they had become used to.

'As a result, the ailing Travises sent the maid and I to be looked after by Ransom's half-brother, William, until I was ready to leave home. That was the first time I met William, who incidentally, was the result of an affair between Ransom's father and one of the white servants. The nature of his birth meant that he lived with his mother in another part of the state, and took a different surname in return for a not ungenerous annual stipend from the Travis family. Anyway, my moving to live with William's family was part of a deal which enabled William to get his hands on the bulk of their fortune, raised from the sale of the plantation. He married his current wife, the daughter of a railroad baron. It was a marriage of convenience for William and his father-in-law. The father-in-law was able to marry off his frumpy, not very pretty daughter, and persuaded William to invest a not inconsiderable sum from his inheritance, in the railroad. In return, William learned the railroad business, resulting in him turning a small fortune into a large one.

'William, incidentally, was a distant figure in my life, but he was kind and generous. The downside of that generosity was that I learnt very few essential life skills, those skills which could enable a woman to survive in the west. I was able to embroider a tapestry and play some classical pieces on the piano, but I didn't know how to cook, work the land or run a homestead. I stayed with William and his wife for seven years until I was twenty-one.

'I was extremely grateful for all the help I had been given, but I had reached an age where I felt ready to leave and seek my own way in the world. Bolstered by an annual stipend from William, I survived very well until my stipend ceased, once I reached the age of twenty-five.

'I had had various suitors but they were too foppish as far as I was concerned, especially knowing from my childhood that the best protector would be a man who was far more worldly and knew how to take care of those he loved. I hung on and hung on for Mr Right, but my savings started to run low. I didn't want to go back to the governor for assistance because I felt that would be like slapping him in the face for all the help he had given me, and telling him that it hadn't been enough.

'Unable to find my Mr Right, I decided that my best option was a marriage of convenience, and seriously started to look for a husband. I was very attractive, and thanks to the governor, exuded style and breeding — an alluring combination for a man of any class.

'As luck (or in the longer term, fate) would decree, I was rescued from the potential ravages of the street by a charming, apparently well-heeled man.

We married, but the marriage was ill conceived because my husband turned out to be no more than a chancer: a gambler and a con man. And of course when his money ran out and his debts started accumulating, I had no choice but to leave him.

'So there I was at the age of thirty-one, a single woman and penniless. I could have worked the street, but I knew I was worth far more than that. So I decided to swallow my pride and plead for the governor's support. Given that in the past, there wasn't really any personal relationship between us, and William being more like an acquaintance in his role as benefactor, he felt the slate was clean for us to start over, but on a different basis, with me becoming his mistress, a kept woman.

'The arrangement worked well initially, and I hoped that over time we could grow to love each other. But after a while I started to see my life as being unfulfilled and compromised by a set of cheap, tacky shackles that prevented me realizing any potential I may have had. With no way out, I began to turn to drink and drugs — a slow journey along the deceptive but seductive road to oblivion. All relationships between a man and a woman are a compromise, and the compromise I had to make was to provide William with the services that a man would normally expect from his wife, and maintain a respectable position in the community, while keeping a public distance from him.

'Of late, of course, he has started talking of marriage in the knowledge that his first wife is dying. But like that loveless relationship, all William really wants is another marriage of convenience, but this time with me playing the role of trophy wife.

'He has given me some choices about other areas of my life, however, such as allowing me to run the local temperance society. I don't have to do that, but William fell in love with the idea of portraying me as a woman of high virtue, who discouraged others in the abuse of their minds and bodies. It complemented the political image he was trying to create of himself: of being not just an upstanding citizen, but an outstanding one — a man of high morals, a leader whom not only the good and the great would naturally want to follow, but in whom the weak and the downtrodden could find inspiration. Unfortunately, although I was able to maintain such an image in public, I was not always able to be the same honourable person in private! Oh, and there is one last thing.' Sarah got up from the table and took some papers out of her desk drawer.

'This is typical of William,' she explained, passing the papers across to Floyd. 'This is a contractual arrangement between William and myself defining the extent of my current role in his life.' Floyd flicked through the papers.

'There's quite a lot of barren land in Russen that William has put in your name,' he pointed out. She shrugged her shoulders.

'I don't know,' she said. 'One thing's for sure, that it won't be for my benefit. It will be for William's, somehow or another.'

'It certainly sounds that he's goin' to be in no hurry to let you go, either, until he's realized his investment,' Floyd said.

'Exactly,' Sarah said. 'William uses the people in his life in all sorts of different ways. But there. I am done!'

'I am very sorry that you have had to relive all that because of me,' Floyd said empathetically. 'That must have been very difficult.'

'No, not at all. It's been a release to share it with someone,' Sarah replied. 'So that is the person my benefactor actually is — but now you are going to tell me that he is somebody different?'

'I'm afraid so,' said Floyd. 'But first let me explain my interest in all of this, an' tell you about my cousin.'

★   ★   ★

'What!' Sarah exclaimed. 'Let me check my understanding is correct. The grave of Ransom Travis had no body in it, whereas there was a skeleton in William Peters' grave? And Emmett Aldstone's evidence supporting Travis's testimony is flawed because he couldn't possibly have seen what he claimed to see? That implies that I have really been sleeping with Captain Ransom Travis, the murderer of my blood family!'

'That's correct,' said Floyd softly. Sarah looked at her empty gin glass and the half full bottle. Suddenly, she grabbed hold of the bottle and threw it against the wall, causing it to smash and shower gin-covered broken glass all over the floor.

'Get me out of here, Floyd!' she screamed. 'Please, take me with you!'

16

'What's the matter, William?' Over all the time they had known each other, Ervine had never seen William look so low. He had walked back into his office to find William sitting there waiting for him and looking very dejected. He had seen him look down before, but never quite like this: down and almost out — or was he?

'Sarah has left me, the bitch!' William said angrily, slapping the palm of his hand down hard on Ervine's desk. 'After everything I've done for her. Ungrateful little whore!'

'I'm mighty sorry to hear that, William,' Ervine said nervously. They had spoken about many things over the years, but never about their relationships with women. 'D'yer know where she's gone? D'yer wan' me to go after her?'

'No,' said William in a resigned voice, 'No. I know where she's gone. She was seen leaving town on the ferry with Greenburn. They'd have gone to Denton.'

'Greenburn, eh. We've had our suspicions about him fer a while. Are yer sure yer don' wan' me . . . '

'No!' interrupted William. 'Not just yet. All in good time. We still need Greenburn to work for us at the moment. This Cove, Faux-Port problem isn't over yet, you know. Bart's hopping mad that his bully boys were completely humiliated by Greenburn. He'll be seeking his revenge, and Greenburn's the only man who can see that we come out of that as the winners. And you know what really gets under my skin about all this?' William said, banging his hand down flat again, on Ervine's desk.

'No, what's that, boss?' Ervine asked, always feeling one step behind the state governor.

'Sarah's taken her copy of the agreement I drew up between us, with her. It's missing from where she normally keeps it.'

'So?' Ervine asked. 'An agreement is an agreement, don't make no difference as to where it is kept.'

'There is a slight complication in the case of this particular agreement,' William pointed out. 'You see, I put a lot of land in Sarah's name. If she has her copy of our agreement she can use it to show title, and then sell it of her own free will.'

'What land is that?' Ervine asked.

'All those plots by the trail that goes north out of Russen.'

'But that ain't worth a light,' Ervine remarked. 'It's barren.'

'Ain't worth a light today, Ervine, but build a railroad next to it and its price will go through the ceiling. I was hoping to see an upward movement in it already, with the public anticipating a Russen victory in the county seat election, but with Marlin Bart creating trouble, I guess people are still sitting on the fence.'

'So how were you ever goin' to get Sarah to relinquish title to that land and hand it back to you?'

'Easy. When my wife dies, which won't be long now, I planned to marry Sarah. After a respectable period of grieving, naturally.'

'I see,' said Ervine. 'So that all depends on whether she might still wanna do that. Why did you put it in her name in the first place, and not buy it in your own?'

'That's due to that strange activity called politics, Ervine. Now, you as mayor could have bought the land in your own name and the public wouldn't have had an issue with that. In fact, such a move would enhance your credibility with them. They would have regarded that as putting your money where your mouth is. A big show of confidence in the town of which you are mayor, and its ability to win the county seat election. But as state governor I can't afford to do that. I have to be seen as neutral. If I had bought the land in my own name, the public would have seen that as me trying to manipulate the election result for my own ends. It's tough, because I know, as a railroad man, that Russen is the natural transport hub of this county, and consequently the only sensible place from which to build any kind of network. It's one of the downsides of high office, Ervine. Sarah was going to be my hedge bet.

'It's a bit of a mess at the moment, isn't it?'

'So what's the plan?' Ervine asked, frustrated that they controlled so little of the situation. 'Do we have one? I mean, should we at least go and get the agreement back? It won't do your image much good if she goes blabbing about all of this. Should we just write her off and kill her? And another thought: what happens if Faux-Port gets so overrun by miners that Green-burn gets killed and we lose our star witness? Should we call in the National Guard to prevent that from happening?'

He paused to let William digest his suggestions.

'Mm, you've got me thinking, Ervine,' William said. 'You know, we actually have a lot more control over this situation than first meets the eye. Do you reckon' you're a better gunfighter than Greenburn? Could you take him on in a duel, say, and win?' Ervine grinned.

'Don't doubt it fer a moment, boss,' he said, laughing.

'Good. Try this for a plan, then,' said William. 'First, we can stop Faux-Port being overrun by miners. We don't need to call in the National Guard. If it looks like it's going to be overrun, we just suspend the rope ferry so they can't get across the river. Anyway, regardless of who wins the battle between Faux-Port and Grainger's Cove, we make sure that Greenburn has sufficient support, to allow him to provide us with evidence that the locals have been intimidated to vote against their will by the Cove thugs. Then we produce this evidence in court, and have a second election ratified, if necessary, at which point Greenburn becomes expendable.

'The result of the court case will be the catalyst for driving up the land prices, so we will need to kidnap Sarah just before then to prevent her from selling the land in her own right. We then use her as bait to lure Greenburn to us. Regardless of whether Greenburn did steal Marson's file from the chest or not, you go to arrest him for it. As a result, and this is the really clever bit, you end up having a gunfight with him, which of course you win.'

'Why's that the really clever bit?' Ervine asked, curious as to why putting his life on the line should be regarded as the 'clever bit'.

'Because it will change Sarah's perception of Greenburn. If we shoot him in cold blood, she will forever see him as a martyr. But this way, she will see him for what he really is: a man who, having been accused of committing a criminal offence, then tries to resist arrest and as a result, loses his life in a fair gunfight. After a brief period of grieving, Sarah will soon come to realize that yet again, I am her only salvation.'

'You make it sound so easy, William,' Ervine commented, sounding almost bemused.

'And you need to make it look as easy as it sounds. Because that's what I pay you for, Ervine. You've never let me down in the past, and I trust you won't this time, either.'

17

Sarah had been settled in Denton for a week and was coming to terms with a new life. Floyd had given her her own log cabin and a job in the invoicing department of his company, as she was insistent on paying her way. It was a strange new cocktail of emotions for her: the giddy, pleasurable feeling from being able to enjoy a new-found freedom, but marred by the occasional fear that William Peters might suddenly exact his revenge in some unknown way. So as far as possible she immersed herself in her work in the invoice department, which acted as a distraction from any fears she was harbouring and kept her grounded. And it was her eye for detail in her new work that caused her to bring to Floyd's attention what appeared to be an irregularity.

'I've been comparing current invoices for the Cove Harbour account with earlier ones,' she told him, 'to make sure that I am processing them correctly, and there appears to be a dramatic change in the type of wood they are ordering. Normally the majority of their orders are for hardwood, but of late they appear to be ordering large quantities of softwood. Is that correct, or have I missed something?'

'Let's see,' said Floyd, looking over her shoulder at the paperwork. 'They would use predominantly hardwood for areas that are exposed and where longevity is required, such as the jetties and boathouses. Softwood would be used for things like pit props, which wouldn't normally be purchased on the harbour account, or the insides of buildings. It's a good spot, Sarah. You're certainly not doing it wrong, and I agree with you that on the surface of it, it does look a little odd. More than a little odd, I would say. Mm. I jest wonder.'

★　★　★

'Shall we moor up here?' Russ asked. There was neither moon nor stars that night, so the main navigation aid was the lights of the buildings.

'Yes,' Floyd agreed. 'We can pull the boat up on to the beach. The tide's goin' out, and this little mission will long be over and us out of here before it comes back in again.' They walked along the shoreline keeping as close to the shadows as possible until they reached the harbour area, where it became easy to mingle with the other boatmen, the merchants and the drunks. At this point they agreed to split up, with Floyd choosing to sniff around the boatyards while Russ went to one of the busier waterfront saloons to see what he could pick up from eavesdropping various conversations at the bar.

★　★　★

'Sorry, mister,' the big Irishman said as he drunkenly barged into Russ, knocking Russ's drink to the ground. 'Buy yer another one.'

'No, it's OK,' said Russ not wanting to attract unnecessary attention. 'Don't worry about it.'

'No, 'tis not,' said the Irishman, holding on to the bar to steady himself. 'Bar keep!' he shouted out. 'Bottle of yer best fer me friend here.' The bar keeper put a bottle of whiskey on the counter for Russ and the Irishman handed over the money.

'You only broke a glass, not a bottle,' Russ protested.

'That's no problem,' the Irishman said. 'It's my treat. Here, I'll help yer out.' He topped up his own glass from the bottle. 'I'm flush with cash tonight, mister. Had a good evenin' so far.'

'Yer won on the tables?' Russ asked.

'Dat's right,' the Irishman nodded. 'Only been here a few days an' I managed to pick up a week's work startin' tomorrow, election week, yer know?'

'Yeah, I sure do,' Russ replied.

'Five dollars a day I'll be gettin' paid, for the whole of dat week. Good money dat is, mister. Would never have got anythin' like dat, back home. So, on the strength o' dat, I decided to invest a little bit o' me savins on the faro table, and won. Money comes to money, dat's what dey say, mister, an' I agree wid 'em.'

'So, what yer gotta do to earn yer five dollars a day?' Russ asked, concerned that someone was trying to stare him down from the other side of the bar.

'The fella who was signin' us up, did say. He used some fancy language to describe it. Nice man though, I quite took to him. Pleasant, he was. A Cornishman. Conway MacPherson was his name. D'yer know 'im?'

'No, can't say as I do,' Russ lied. He had noticed out of the corner of his eye, that the man who had been trying to stare him down had moved, and was making his way towards the side of the bar where Russ and the Irishman were talking.

'Now what was we sayin' before we spoke about dat Conway?' the Irishman asked.

'I was askin' yer about what yer had to do fer five dollars a day.' The man with the stare came and stood next to the Irishman and pulled out a knife.

'I gotta score to settle with you, pal,' he said to Russ, interrupting the conversation. 'You're one of those three guys who made me walk fer miles in me stocking feet, the other week. No one makes me look stupid an' lives to tell the tale. No one!' The Irishman tapped Russ's would-be assailant on the shoulder, who instinctively turned around — and met the Irishman's elbow which hit him full in the face, shattering his nose.

'Wait yer turn, mister,' the Irishman ordered the assailant. 'We were talkin'.' The last words were wasted on the assailant, who hit the floor unconscious and remained that way as his buddies lifted him up under the arms and dragged him outside.

'Thanks fer that,' Russ said.

'Oh, dat's OK, mister. Tink nothin' of it. Can't stand bad manners. Makes me angry.' The Irishman poured himself another drink. 'There,' he said. 'Dis will calm me down. Now, ah yes! Canvassin', dat's the word.'

'What word?' Russ asked.

'The fancy word, dat Conway used to describe what we'd be doin' in Faux-Port.'

'Faux-Port?' Russ queried.

'Yes. It's across the river, over there,' the Irishman said, pointing in entirely the wrong direction. 'I can tell you're new to these parts, mister. D'yer know what it means?'

'What, what means?'

'Canvassin',' the Irishman replied, plonking himself down on a nearby stool. Russ shook his head, knowing full well that the Irishman couldn't wait to tell him. 'Well, it means we're to try and persuade the people of Faux-Port as to why they should vote for the Cove.'

'An' how do yer go about this canvassin'?' Russ asked.

'Dat's simple. By whatever means it takes. Yer see, when the votes from Faux-Port are counted, fer every vote fer the Cove, the canvassin' team, as a group, gets awarded half a pint of whiskey, which will be doubled if the Cove wins the election. So, we won't be takin' 'no' fer an answer! There's gonna be dozens of us doin' this, so it should be quite a party atmosphere.' The Irishman stopped briefly to replenish his glass, thirsty at the thought of it all.

'In fac',' he said, sounding drunker and drunker, 'there's goin' to be an arm er, armer, no — an armada of us, that's it!' And with that, he leant back and fell off his stool, landing on the floor in a drunken heap.

'Hey, mister,' the bar keeper called out to Russ. 'Help me shift him into the corner. He can sleep it off there without bein' disturbed. Seems like a regular

214

drinker to me, an' in this business, it pays to look after yer regulars.'

★   ★   ★

'Anythin' else, mister?' the butcher asked. 'Want some of that steak cooked?'

'No thanks, prefer it raw.' Floyd handed payment for the meat. He'd bought enough for eight large meals. The street seller wrapped the meat in a piece of cloth and passed it to Floyd, who put it in a leather messenger bag. He walked along the edge of the harbour, past the stalls where traders were selling everything from medicines, cloth, fresh fish, cooked fish, fresh coffee, meat and vegetables. The place was vibrant, alive with optimism, a thriving secondary economy, underwritten almost entirely on hope — the hope of finding gold. Floyd made one last purchase, a small bottle of laudanum, before he left this crowded area and made for the back of the cove.

Unlike in the daytime, it was dark and quiet there, now. For this was the area where the boats unloaded the supplies that enabled Grainger's Cove to function: food, medicine, drink, tools, building equipment and so on. The buildings were mainly warehouses where all these items were stored until required for use. In addition there were the normal buildings you would expect in the 'business quarter' of a small town, such as the bank, the assay office, the claims office, the livery stables and the blacksmith's shop. Floyd wasn't interested in any of these, however: his destination was the boatyard beyond all these other buildings.

Once he arrived, he soon discovered that a number of changes had been made since his last visit, as others had mentioned. An eight-foot high barbed-wire fence had been installed around the perimeter of the yard. This meant that although it was still possible to see what was going on, no one could walk in and inspect the activities closely. At night, the four wolf-like guard dogs were no longer chained to the watchman's hut as they had always been, but were now free to roam wherever they wanted inside the barbed-wire enclosure. Under-nourished to keep them mean and hungry, the dogs' preferred choice was to stay near the night-watchman's hut, since he was their recognized supplier of food and water, however meagre the portions and irregular the delivery.

There was a slight breeze so Floyd made sure he was downwind of the dogs, to minimize the chance of them picking up his scent. He laid his messenger bag on the ground and crouching down, removed the four items inside. First, he unwrapped four of the eight raw steaks and threw them as far as he could into the enclosure, between the strands of wire. The dogs got up one by one and padded over to the midnight feast that had just landed in their enclosure, sniffed around it and started to eat hungrily.

Floyd then rolled up his left shirt sleeve, removed the metal vambrace from his bag — another piece of armour that Dan, the blacksmith, had made for him — and placed it over his forearm, and rolled his shirtsleeve down over it. This was his first line of defence if one of the dogs attacked: he would offer up his metal-covered forearm and let the dog try and bite through it, which would give him the chance to cuff it hard on its very sensitive nose with the butt of his gun. If the creature proved too resilient, or if one of the other dogs tried to attack at the same time, then he would have to open fire, but he really wanted to avoid the extra attention that might bring. Next, he cut the bottom strand of the barbed wire fence and crawled through the gap into the enclosure.

The night watchman was dozing by the side of his brazier, a half-empty whiskey bottle by his side. Floyd took out his Remington, and holding the end of the barrel against the watchman's temple, pulled back the hammer.

'Go call the dogs back and chain them up. Give them this for their trouble,' he said, offering the watchman the second set of raw steak. 'I'll be watchin' yer from the safety of your hut here. If you try an' set one of those dogs on me, the bullet from this gun will take you out first and the second bullet will take the dog out. Understan'?' The watchman nodded. Floyd watched him from the small window. The dogs, more interested in the extra steaks, came over straightaway and allowed their minder to chain them to the hut.

'I've topped up yer whiskey bottle,' he said as the watchman came back inside.

'I dunno what yer game is, mister, but I don't wan' no trouble. Too tired fer that.'

'Good,' said Floyd. 'You've made the right decision. Treat yerself to another drink.' The combination of the whiskey and the laudanum soon had the watchman snoring his head off. Floyd cautiously stepped outside. The dogs were snoozing as well.

★ ★ ★

'Did yer find anythin'?' Russ asked Floyd as they pushed their boat back into the water and quietly rowed into the River Russen.

'Sure did,' Floyd replied. 'After I'd taken care of the watchman an' his dogs, I was able to take a look around the boatyard. Our softwood is there. They've used it to build rafts. Each one big enough to ferry I guess about ten people. They've built twenty already, an' I reckon they have enough wood stock piled up to build quite a few more.'

'Enough to move at least two hundred people. That's a fair-sized armada.'

'Armada?' queried Floyd.

'Yep,' Russ replied. 'I got talkin' to some drunken Irishman. Bart's payin' the miners to go to Faux-Port in election week an' canvas support fer the Cove. Sounds like a potential ugly situation to me.'

'Does, don't it? Could end up with a false election result and a bloodbath.'

'Does Fulbeck still wan' us to police Faux-Port?' Russ asked as he started to think about the various scenarios.

'Yes, he does,' Floyd replied. 'Tol' me that the governor still sees no reason to call in the National Guard. Reckoned that if there was a mass crossin' they'd suspend the rope ferry.'

'He's obviously no idea of what Bart an' MacPherson are plannin', otherwise he'd change his mind.'

'Too late now, anyway,' Floyd pointed out. 'If your Irishman's right, an' I expect he is — drunken men can ferget many things, but never when the next pay day is — it means that two hundred miners could easily be entrenched in Faux-Port by tomorrow lunchtime. Take two or three days to mobilize the National Guard at least.'

'So in the meantime, how do we get the people of Faux-Port to defend their rights? They ain't fightin' people?'

'We can't,' said Floyd. 'It could be done, but there ain't enough time. It's as simple as that. Many of 'em have probably got the gun skills to hit a movin' target, but it's the time it'll take for them to change their attitude — to learn how to harden their mind so they're not afraid to look the enemy in the eye an' kill 'em. And once it's all over, to be able to realize that what they did was just and honourable, an' that the god of them an' their people was on their side. No, our only hope is to prevent the armada from landing, if we can!'

18

Floyd reasoned that the miners' armada wouldn't set sail until mid-morning at the earliest, but more likely after lunch. After all, if he were Marlin Bart, he would have wanted his army of intimidators to arrive in Faux-Port feeling more than a little dour and grumpy, basically like bears with sore heads. Normally it would take those who had had a heavy night the night before until mid-morning just to come around, let alone start to come to terms with their hangovers.

So as dawn broke, Floyd's lumber operation came alive. Several hundred large logs were piled up by the top of the flume and then loaded on, and sent down the flume to the river bank, where men piled them up again as they came off the end. And as the sun appeared above the horizon, Chancy and his small team of log drivers stood on the logs wearing their spiked boots and started guiding them downstream, using just the current of the river and long wooden poles with a metal spike on one end. Their plan was simple. Using the small group of navigational 'marker' rocks that protruded from the middle of the river south of Grainger's Cove, their aim was to jam the logs in and around this group of rocks, effectively building a dam across the river and thus preventing traffic from moving down- or upstream. Having executed that part of the plan, a boom would be made by driving sharp, pointed hooks into the log ends and attaching short chains, and the boom would then be thrown around the dam to keep it in place.

Having done that, they made another boom, to secure a six-foot wide loose raft of timber against the west bank of the river and extending northwards, from the dam to Denton. The strategic purpose of the first boom was to prevent the miners' armada sailing far enough south to reach Faux-Port, and the purpose of the second one was to prevent them pursuing an alternative route by landing on the west bank and walking south to Faux-Port along the Denton trail. Effectively it was a containment strategy, restricting the armada to its home town harbour, if needs be until after the county seat election was over. As the miners were waking up, nursing their hangovers, the booms were in place.

'Well done, boys. Yer done it with time to spare,' Floyd said congratulating the driver crews. 'Any problems?' he asked Chancy.

'Only one,' Chancy said. 'When we were out by the rocks in the middle of the river there was a small rowin' boat wedged in between 'em. Looked a bit strange. On closer inspection we saw it had been holed beneath the waterline. Inside we found the body of a woman, tied down with stones in her clothin' an' a bullet hole through the centre of her forehead. I know you've got a better, quality replacement now, but we found this in one of her pockets.' Chancy handed Floyd his tin deputy's badge.

'The badge I left with Marietta as a deposit. So, it must have been her?'

'Couldn't say fer certain 'cos the body wasn't in a good state, but I guess it must have been,' Chancy replied.

★ ★ ★

'Do you think your defences will be sufficient, Sheriff Greenburn?' Michel Rousseau asked.

'They should be very effective, but we need an offensive strategy as well, if we are to win the war.'

'You mean using fighters, don't you? That doesn't come naturally to us. You saw how my son reacted when his mother told him to shoot Perez. He just couldn't do it, not even to save his father's life, and my son's a very good shot!'

'No, I don't mean fighters. All I need are posturers,' Floyd said, reflecting on Michel's son's reaction and what he himself had learnt from the Civil War.

'Posturers? I don't understand.'

'When you're under attack, there's a choice of four responses. You can choose to fight, you can run away, you can give in, or you can posture. It's actin' like you're a fighter, even if you're not. The aim is to frighten the enemy, make 'em think that your bite is gonna be a whole lot worse than your bark. That's what I mean by posturin'. Trust me, it can be very effective. How many people have felt scared at the sound of an Indian war cry? Most everyone, an' how many people have been scared enough to flee, if the war cry is loud enough and curdles the blood? Many, I can tell you.'

'So, you want us to do this posturing so that the miners decide it's just too difficult to take on the people of Faux-Port?'

'Exactly, Michel.'

'So, what would it involve? How would we do it?'

'All I would need is thirty of your best shooters, armed with rifles. The miners will definitely try and sail across, and will attempt to break through the log jam we have created. All I want you folks to do is to posture by shooting over their heads. They won't know that that's what you're doin' — they'll think it's fer real. It'll frighten 'em, make 'em believe they're livin' on borrowed time. If we need some more accurate shootin' to convince 'em the threat is real, then my men will provide that.' Floyd could see Michel thinking over this idea.

'OK,' Michel said. 'We'll do it. It's a deal.'

★ ★ ★

It wasn't until mid-afternoon that the first dozen rafts left the Cove harbour in single file. The miners on board were not a particularly disciplined bunch, and some had already started drinking again, regarding the whole affair as nothing but a paid holiday. From the forested ledges up above the Denton trail, where Michel and his men started to open fire, it was quite an amusing spectacle. The rafts sailed out into the River Russen and turned south, ready to steer a diagonal course across the river to Faux-Port. As they reached the 'marker' rocks and the dam of logs, they were forced to turn west in an attempt to land on the bank by the Denton Trail, only to find this route impeded by another logjam that hugged the side of the bank going north, as far as the eye could see.

And so the whole armada, maintaining its single-file formation, went around in a big circle and sailed back into the harbour.

★ ★ ★

'That bastard Greenburn's done me agen!' Marlin Bart screamed. 'I'll swing fer him, I will,' he shouted. 'An' what about our men, what did they make of it?'

'I think their main concern is that they will lose a day's pay,' Conway MacPherson replied.

'Too damned right, they will!' Bart screamed. 'They've achieved nothin' today, so why should I pay 'em?'

'I think if you don't, they might not carry on. You promised to pay 'em daily, an' as far as they are concerned your word is your bond, Mr Bart, sir. They don't see it as their fault that Greenburn's decided to jam up the river with his logs.'

'You're right there, MacPherson. Greenburn's created a damned logjam. An' d'yer know how yer get rid of one of those quickly? Do yer?'

'No, Mr Bart, sir,' Conway replied.

'Dynamite, Conway. An' lots of it. But it's a new moon at present an' this ain't a job to be done in the dark. Needs to be carefully placed, like it does when makin' a mine shaft. You'll have to do it by daylight, somehow. Just keep throwin' dynamite at those dam logs until they get movin'! If I know Greenburn, he ain't gonna shoot to kill a man who's breakin' up his logjam. And every man who turns up at sunrise tomorrow will get paid for today! You tell 'em, Conway!'

★   ★   ★

'I tink he's mad, Conway.'

'Who yer talkin' about, Irish?' Conway asked.

'Yer know, yer man. The boss man. That Marlin feller.'

'Why?'

'Dese logs. They're all held in place by de booms, an' they're chained together. Look at dat dam.' Their raft, the lead raft of the convoy, was about one hundred yards away from the north side of the dam. 'We'd need to blow a gap in de boom on de south side of de dam first, so dat the logs flow out, downstream. An' to do dat, we'd have to clamber over de loose logs inside the boom. It's too far to throw a stick from de raft, standin' on a wet, movin' surface.'

'So?'

'Well, I ain't doin' it. Those log drivers make it look easy, walkin' on wet logs as dey float up an' down an' roll in the current, but I can assure yer it ain't. Easier to walk on the damned water!'

'Ok, I'll get someone else to do it.'

'I'll do it fer yer, boyo. I'll have a go.'

'Thanks, Taffy,' said Conway.

'Well, they ain't shootin' at us terday. I wouldn't wanna do it if they were.'

'That's true they're not,' said Irish. 'I still don't like the sound of it. They're up to somethin', to be sure!' he exclaimed. They brought the raft alongside the northern edge of the dam and held it steady, long enough for Taffy to crawl off on to the boom.

A stick of dynamite and a roll of fuse wire in his pockets, he felt like a man on a mission. The loose logs inside the boom were too far apart to crawl over, so he would have to walk. As he steadily got to his feet, a cheer went up from the raft. Taffy took two successful steps, invoking louder cheers. His confidence levels boosted not least by the rousing vocal support of his colleagues, Taffy took a longer third step. As he placed his leading foot on the log in front of him and started to place his weight on it, the log rose up slightly out of the water and rotated on its axis. Taffy rotated his arms backwards, faster and faster, to try and keep his balance. But it was too late. He fell backwards into the water, submerged briefly and as he came back up, two logs crashed against his head, which became the filling in a wood sandwich. The cracking of his skull could be heard aboard the raft, and he lost consciousness just before he died.

* * *

'How many rafts have turned back?' Floyd asked. Russ raised the telescope to his eye.

'Jest three, that's all. The three behin' Conway's. The others seem to be sailin' towards the boom which runs down the west bank by the Denton Trail.'

'Maybe they're jest gonna throw all their dynamite at it an' blitz their way through. OK, I'm fed up with this. Let's start releasin' the rest of the logs.'

★ ★ ★

The miners were quick to learn. They were never afraid to try something new, and if that idea didn't yield results, they were focused and innovative in modifying it somehow, so that it did work. So now, being forced to pursue their second choice of landing place, the Denton Trail, they were able to wedge sticks of dynamite in the chains that held the boom together, without stepping foot off the rafts, and then shot at the sticks to ignite them, from a safe distance away. After about ten minutes' shooting they had managed to breach part of the boom in three different places.

'We've done it, Irish,' shouted Conway, looking at the freed logs, now out in the main current and floating past their raft. The men on board cheered again.

'You ain't cheerin', Irish!' Conway exclaimed. One of the reasons why Irish preferred being drunk to sober was that when he was sober he often found that his 'take' on a situation was different from others, and that invariably, he was the one who was right — even though there was little satisfaction in going against the grain of public opinion. And this was another of those situations, and the frustration of it was enough to drive a man like Irish, to drink.

'We didn't release all these logs, to be sure,' he pointed out. 'These are new ones. Greenburn's releasin' more of 'em upstream and eventually they're gonna pile up against that dam jest south of us that poor Taffy couldn't breach. An' yer know what that means, don't yer?'

'Go on,' said Conway.

'If we don't get back into the Cove pretty quick, our rafts are gonna be stuck on this damned river in an almighty logjam! I jest hope we got plenty of drink stashed away at the harbour, 'cos it could take days to sort this mess out — days without any new supplies bein' able to get through!'

★ ★ ★

'This feels like the end, Conway. For now, at least, until I come up with another idea.' Marlin Bart drew heavily on his cigar as he paced the length of his lounge. 'I've underestimated Greenburn, an' as a result we're likely to lose the county seat election. All that extra revenue lost. I dunno what to do, right now.'

'I think yer should go, Mr Bart.'

'Pardon, Conway. What did yer say?'

'I said, I think yer should go. Listen, outside.' Conway pointed at the window. Bart strode across the room, and stood

behind the velvet curtain, cautiously peer-
ing around it.

'It's a bayin' mob. They're carryin' a
noose! Who have they come for?'

'You, Mr Bart. They've come for
you.'

'Do somethin', Conway! Stop 'em!'

'I don't know if I can, Marlin. Like I
couldn't stop 'em when they came for
Ezra Danneville, remember?' Marlin
nodded nervously. 'You see, you've
gone too far this time. You've offended
their dignity — an' mine, fer that
matter, by takin' advantage of us fer yer
own ends. If it weren't fer them, you
wouldn't be here. An' thanks to them,
you ain't gonna be here much longer.
But I haven't forgotten what you've
done fer me, either. At heart, I've
always seen merself as an honourable
man. So if you leave now by the back
door, I've left a fast horse there for yer.
I can calm 'em by tellin' 'em that
you've already made yer getaway an'
have sworn never to step foot in these
parts agen. They trust me, yer see, an' I

will not break that trust, which I have earned from such a fine body of men. But the same cannot be said fer you.'

19

'Well, surprise, surprise, eh Ervine?' William said with a big smile on his face. 'I think it's fair to say that Greenburn's done us proud. By this time next week we'll be celebrating the fact that not only has Russen retained the county seat, but as a result, I can start building my cherished railroad.' He walked to the drinks cabinet and poured two glasses of whiskey.

'I guess Greenburn has, William, I guess he has. Not only that, but he has given us an unexpected bonus with Bart being forced into exile. A nasty piece of work, if ever there was one. A man who builds empires directly off other people's backs. Empires based on hope, yet made of sand. No one could say that about us, William.'

'Indeed not,' said William, passing Ervine his drink. 'The opposite, in fact.

You know, many railroad barons operate in exactly the same way as Bart
does. They build a railroad wherever
they think they can make a quick
operational profit for themselves, and
stuff the investor. Most of these
schemes are just not going to last.
Short-term profit requiring long-term
investment. It's a scam. My schemes
are not like that. They are not about a
quick buck. Mine are all about
long-term investment for long-term
profit. Where the trails and the
waterways are more competitive, we
integrate with them. We don't try and
force them out of business because
we're on a power lack. It's about the
bigger picture, where we can all get a
fair return on our contribution, and the
big winners are the communities. You
know Ervine, I was explaining this to
President Cleveland the other week,
and he was quite smitten!'

Ervine stifled a yawn and tried to stay
engaged. He had heard this egocentric
rhetoric from William so often, it had

become boring. But on the other hand, he had often found that when you had picked the rhetoric apart and taken off the wrapping paper, the parcel inside had more than its fair share of substance, unlike the claims of many other egotists.

'So where do we stand with Greenburn?' Ervine asked, having felt he had paid sufficient homage to his boss's quest for admiration.

'Well, I think that for the greater good, it remains the same,' said William. 'We take Sarah back, then we get rid of Greenburn. I feel slightly saddened that I have to reach that conclusion, but in terms of the future and that greater good, I'm afraid I struggle to see where Greenburn will fit in. He has indeed made an honourable contribution, but he has, alas, now served his purpose. And that, dear Ervine, will be the triple prize for surviving these last few wearisome days: Sarah subservient to me again, Greenburn dead, and

Russen once more the democratically elected county seat holder. Everything that directly follows as a consequence will just be nature taking its true and just course. Do you agree?' Ervine couldn't be bothered even to comment, but just nodded obediently.

★ ★ ★

As Floyd strolled through the forest, he could hear the occasional sound of a blast of dynamite in the distance as his men cleared the logjams. The river was running free again as a result, and the floating lumber guided to Faux-Port harbour where it was being hauled out of the water and stockpiled on the quayside. With the Greenburn workforce away downstream, opening up the river for the various cargo and leisure boats to apply their trade once more, Floyd found it possible to hear himself think in the forests of Denton, which were temporarily unencumbered from the noise of lumberjacks and their equipment.

It was the relative silence, the ability to feel part of nature again, that allowed his thoughts to follow their own course — and they presented him with a startling revelation as to the possible identity and whereabouts of Emmett Aldstone, the army captain who claimed to have witnessed, at least in part, the atrocity that happened in Honer County in 1861, and whose evidence absolved Captain Ransom Travis from any blame for the slaughter of unarmed citizens. Floyd stopped, taken aback. The idea appeared to fit the facts, as far as anyone knew or understood them, but any accusations were bound to be denied or rebuffed without more compelling evidence.

As he started to walk on again, wondering how he might be able to resolve that dilemma, his thinking was interrupted by the sound of gunfire coming from the sawmill area. Floyd raced down the mountainside. As he got closer he could hear the sound of the sawmill steam engine pumping and the circular saw blade spinning around.

Arriving at the back of the mill, six-gun in hand, Floyd was just in time to see Chancy and Russ roll a set of large logs on to one of the gunfighters, knocking him to the ground and pinning him there.

'It's Fulbeck and two of his men!' Russ shouted.

'Take 'em alive, if yer can. I think they can help us,' Floyd shouted back. 'Who turned the mill on?'

'It was Fulbeck,' Chancy said. 'He turned it on so that he could make his getaway, preventing us from climbing over the cradle and track.' A couple of shots whistled across their heads.

'That's the one who is still in there. Fulbeck ordered him to provide coverin' fire.'

'OK,' said Floyd. 'Let's capture him first an' then we can get after Fulbeck.'

Russ and Chancy entered the mill from the south door, while Floyd entered from the north. The track that carried the log cradle to the saw ran east-to-west down the middle of the shed, and Fulbeck's accomplice was now hemmed in by the moving track gear on one side and Chancy and Russ's gunfire on the other. Pinned down and determined not to heed their call to surrender, the gunman realized that he would be in a much better position if he could clamber over the track and its pulley mechanism that moved the log cradle along, and fight just one opposing gun, namely Floyd.

Sensing that either Russ or Chancy was reloading, the gunman let off a couple of shots and climbed on to the moving log cradle, hoping to jump off the other side and seek relative safety behind the boiler pump. But as he tried to jump off, his jacket got caught up on part of the cradle! The man looked at the spinning saw blade fifteen yards away, his eyes stinging from the perspiration rolling off his forehead: if he didn't act quickly, within the next thirty seconds he was going to be sliced in half!

Seeing his predicament, Floyd stood up to make his way to the lever mechanism that would disengage the power to the two moving parts that could cost the man his life: the spinning circular saw blade and the pulley wheel that moved the log cradle and its human cargo towards a gruesome death! Yet as he did so, the man shot at him.

'I'm tryin' to help you!' Floyd shouted out. Twenty seconds to go, but the man couldn't hear him over the clattering and clanging of the equipment. Floyd got up to try again but the frightened man let off another shot. Fifteen seconds to go. From his side of the track, Chancy had a better view. He cocked his gun and aimed. The first bullet missed. Ten seconds to go. Chancy repeated the action. This time his bullet hit the gunman on the wrist, and he dropped his gun. Seven seconds to go. Floyd was up on his feet and raced towards the controls. The first lever switched off the saw, and although the blade started to slow down immediately, it was still turning rapidly under its own momentum. Five seconds to go. The next lever stopped the log cradle, two feet away from the blade. The gunman passed out, and as he fell to the ground, his weight tore his jacket completely so he fell off the log cradle. He stirred as he hit the ground.

'I'll get after Fulbeck!' Floyd shouted to Russ and Chancy.

★   ★   ★

Floyd moved down the slopes as quickly as his sense of caution would allow, ensuring that he maintained as much cover from the trees as possible. As he approached Sarah's cabin he saw the front door had been left open and was gently swinging in the breeze as if it had been abandoned. He went inside, stealthily moving from room to room, and called her name. Nothing. She'd gone!

Leaving the front door swinging he

made his way further down the slope, less cautiously than before. As the cover of the trees retreated he was able to make out the shoreline ahead of him. In the distance he could see two figures climbing into a boat, a man and a woman. He took his telescope from his pocket and raised it to his eye. Ervine Fulbeck and Sarah. They pushed away from the shore with Fulbeck taking charge of the oars. Floyd noted his rowing skills were at best average.

He reasoned they must be making for Russen. He knew they had too great a start for him to catch up with them by boat, but he considered he might be able to get there before them on horseback. He would surely be able to overtake them once he was south of Faux-Port, but whether he could beat them to Russen would depend on where the rope ferry was, and how long he might have to wait to board it.

20

William Peters had a sense of foreboding. He didn't like it. He had very little control over the next few hours and his paranoia was starting to get to him. Ervine Fulbeck had gone to snatch back Sarah, and until she arrived safe and sound, there was nothing he could do but wait, holed up in his hotel room, for a message. He fancied a drink, but it wouldn't do for him, as the state governor and executive trustee of the Temperance Society, to be seen drinking alone in the middle of the day — then he suddenly realized that the Temperance Society was the very place he could help himself to alcohol undisturbed. Sarah had a stash locked away in a cupboard, left behind by those patrons anxious to kick the habit.

He found the key in the place where Sarah always hid it, and opened the cupboard door. Although depleted of gin, there were a few bottles of whiskey, none of it decent stuff, but when a man needs a drink he told himself, then a man needs a drink. As he sat in the room where he had secretly first courted Sarah, glass in hand, he felt all alone. Alone and full of foreboding. It was unlike him. William had only ever felt like this once before, and the emotion brought the memory flooding back to him. It was of the day that he had been arrested on the charge of massacring the population of a small village in 1861.

Even now, he was still paranoid that what people didn't understand then, some still didn't understand today. He recalled his words of explanation to his defence team, his description of how, at the time, the villagers were widely regarded as traitors and that many confederates, himself included, had dehumanized them as a result. And how, when his unit had walked into the village, it had been eerily quiet, as if the population had up and left. He had sensed the worst, that the villagers were still there, armed to the hilt and about to spring a surprise attack. So as soon as he saw movement, he ordered his troops to fire at will. What else could a young man in charge of trained killers be expected to do under the circumstances?

And then, as if the hand of fate decreed it to be so, the circumstances changed.

Wheels within wheels started to turn, witnesses were found, and before long the military tribunal found him not guilty — and this was all thanks to various political power plays. It was then William realized that once he had made his fortune, ultimately, he would like to become a successful politician, because people with power could make things happen. 'Be a winner' was what he used to tell himself, and as he sipped at his cheap whiskey, that was what he told himself now.

After all, he had Ervine running the

show wherever security was required, and who better? Although he often seemed to work under sufferance, Ervine was highly capable, discreet, and immensely loyal. He was paid handsomely for these abilities, of course, but knew his place and his only ambition appeared to be to hang on to William's coat tails and be part of the Peters' success story. The state governor started to feel better.

★   ★   ★

Ervine Fulbeck stared at the woman in front of him. Although not a great oarsman, his stamina enabled him to row tirelessly, maintaining a steady rhythm, for most of the time. The woman, Sarah Tamswaite, sat motionless in the stern of the small boat, her wrists tied in front of her. Ervine wished he had a woman like her for his own. In his line of work, to attract someone with the airs and graces of respectability such as Sarah, was

252

difficult. He had hoped his appointment as Mayor of Russen was about to change all this, and he could at last do something honourable, where he could hold his head high in civil society.

But it seemed that William Peters had other ideas. If so, Ervine would have to keep up the pretence of having made his fortune from gold mining, a lie that seemed to satisfy his remote neighbours who must have wondered why a man with such a comfortable lifestyle never appeared to work. He would have to go on spending hours at shooting practice so he could take out any two-bit gunslinger who crossed William's path without trouble. In short, he would have to continue to be State Governor Peters' secret 'fixer' and hired assassin.

And this was all because as a young man he had accepted a king's ransom to break the law. It was only meant to have been once — a chance to set himself up, an unofficial reward for having to suffer the horrors of war. But under the spell of William Peters, he had found himself having to suffer the horrors of peace. The only way he could deal with being a hired assassin was to emotionally detach himself from his work as much as possible, and in order to preserve what little humanity he had left, dispatch his victims as mercifully as he could.

But today, that was going to change. As he looked into Sarah Tamswaite's eyes, he could see the innocence of her soul, an innocence that he hoped might still be buried somewhere deep within his own. Ervine had always been afraid of walking away from William, afraid that William would see such an action as some sort of betrayal and pay someone else to dispatch the dispatcher! So today, somehow, he had to take control and make that change.

★ ★ ★

Sarah looked away from Ervine Fulbeck's gaze. She was uncomfortable with this horrible man leering at her.

She needed to run through in her mind, how she would behave towards Peters when she saw him again, as she guessed that that was where she was being taken. She didn't anticipate being physically harmed. She expected she would be dealing with a man whose massive ego had been dented, but who was still besotted with her. He would try to woo her back, and if that didn't work, would keep her prisoner until she did. She decided a repetitive strategy of verbal resistance followed by a period of complete silence would be appropriate until Floyd came to rescue her. She refused to contemplate any other scenario.

★ ★ ★

Floyd rode along the Denton trail at speed. He knew that Russ and Chancy would follow on behind as quickly as they could. He had left in a hurry, less prepared than he would have been normally, but that was because Sarah was potentially in great danger. As he rode he contemplated the possible scenarios, and as far as he could see there were only three. First, he assumed that Fulbeck was taking Sarah to Russen. Second, Fulbeck might have some more gunslingers on hand, outnumbering Floyd when he stepped off the rope ferry. He reasoned that this was more likely than the first scenario, but the odds would still be against Fulbeck having time to organize such a welcoming party, if he kept riding fast.

The third scenario was the one he considered the most likely: a gunfight between him and Fulbeck. What he needed to avoid, however, was a duel against such a formidable opponent; a street and alleyway fight using the buildings as cover would give him more chance.

★   ★   ★

'Like I said, you didn't manage to get Greenburn then?' William wanted to hear Ervine admit his failure for a second time.

'No, William. I already told yer that,' Ervine said, determined to show William that he wouldn't rise to the bait. 'It was three of 'em against three of us, an' besides, we had to bring back the woman.'

'Sarah, you mean?'

'Yes, Sarah. I've locked her up in the town jail. She's unharmed. That's what yer really wanned, wasn't it?' William nodded.

'Greenburn's my problem an' I'll take care of it.'

'Yes, he is, but I am surprised you are two men down in the process. Hope you are not losing your touch, Ervine.' His comment was ignored. 'Right, take me to my Sarah.' The two men left Ervine's office in Russen town hall and walked along the street to the jail.

★   ★   ★

'Sarah,' William looked at her longingly. 'You are unharmed, I trust.'

'Yes,' she replied coldly. William

257

signalled to Ervine to unlock her cell and enable him to go to her. She shunned his embrace.

'My wife is definitely dying, Sarah. The doctor says she has just days to go. Do you realize that soon we will be able to formalize our relationship and announce it to the world?'

'State Governor Ransom Travis,' Sarah said coldly. 'There is no relationship between us, and nor will there be. You are not William Peters. He is your half-brother and lies buried in his grave which is next to yours, except that you are not in it, yet! You see, I know all about you. Who you really are and what you really did.'

'Who told you that? It was Green-burn, wasn't it? Is he your new lover?'

'No,' Sarah replied, 'to both your questions.'

'You are lying, Sarah,' William said quietly, in a matter of fact way. Embarrassed, she purposely avoided his gaze. 'My family did many things for you. They took you in, when circumstances made you an orphan, and gave you a passport to a life of opportunity. A life that you otherwise would not have had. A privileged education in the arts and the sciences, for example. In return you were brought up to show compassion, humility and gratitude. And not to lie, which is what you are trying to do, albeit badly, now. So, it was Greenburn. He must have been the one that stole that damned curator's records from the chest,' he said angrily. He paused to calm himself down. 'I knew it,' he said in a resigned tone, regaining his composure. 'So, where does that leave you and I, Sarah?'

'Where do you think?' said Sarah equally calmly, but a lot more coldly. 'Floyd Greenburn may not be as wealthy as you. He may not have the breeding and airs and graces that you have. He may not be as intelligent as you, or understand as well as you how the political power plays work. But he is a far more honourable man than you are, or will ever be. And in the eyes of an educated lady, who was brought up not to lie and show compassion, humility and gratitude count for everything. For example, why did you feel compelled to take on a different name, if you were innocent of the slaughter of my family, friends and neighbours back in 1861?'

'Because, Sarah, even though I was found not guilty by the court, there were many who still didn't believe that I was innocent. Because of the upbringing we both had at the hands of the Travis family, I had a lot to offer society and needed to be given the chance to prove it. As a consequence, to overcome others' prejudice and lack of faith in our justice system, when the chance came to change my name and take on my dead half-brother's identity, I took it. I don't want to sound big-headed, but I can demonstrate that I have added value to society. Probably the most important, enduring changes that I have made, is thanks to my railroad business. I have created jobs for people and brought distant communities together. I haven't just changed society by doing that, I have transformed it. And that is why, to repay that debt of opportunity and privilege which society has given me, I put myself forward to be the democratically elected state governor and serve the people.

'I have made mistakes. I have my failings, but I am only human. At least, come the day of reckoning, my conscience is clear that I will have done more good in this world than most people, and certainly more good than I will have done bad. My account is currently in credit, and will remain so. And that, my dear Sarah, is because I am an honourable man.'

If his speech was having any positive effect on Sarah, it was having less of one on Ervine.

'You're all washed up, William and yer know it. Finished.' Ervine said. 'The woman and her boyfriend know too much. We follow our normal procedure from now on in. We've always agreed that.'

'No!' William interjected quickly. 'I'll deal with her. I know a safe place where I can talk it all through with her. She'll see sense, I know she will. You do as I say and get out there and deal with Greenburn when he turns up. Otherwise,' William paused momentarily, wondering if he should finish the sentence. 'Otherwise, I will tell her about your past!' But it was too late — the threat was out, as was Ervine's gun. He fanned the hammer back with his left hand and pulled the trigger with his right. Peters fell to the ground and landed on his back. Dead. Sarah stood dumbstruck, looking at the bullet wound in the middle of his forehead.

'Fulbeck! It's Floyd Greenburn! Show yerself wherever you are! I'm outside!' Ervine grabbed hold of the frightened Sarah.

'I'm comin' for yer, Greenburn!' Ervine shouted back. 'I'm gonna come out the jailhouse, right behind Sarah. My gun's in her back, so don't try anythin' stupid!' Floyd kept his hand away from his gun belt as Fulbeck and Sarah appeared in the street. He couldn't risk putting her life in jeopardy.

'Peters is dead, so it's jest you, me, an' the woman now,' Fulbeck continued. 'I guess you wanna kill me, Greenburn, so that you can have the woman an' justify my death by tellin' the world some made-up, exaggerated story about my past. On the other hand, with Peters out of the way, an' in my position as the Mayor of Russen, I can now live an honourable life unimpeded, as I was always meant to. I sure ain't gonna let you come between me an' that, Greenburn. Besides, I've decided I wan' the woman fer merself; a town like this needs a mayor with a wife.

'But I wanna play fair with you, 'cos that's part of my true nature. So I challenge yer to a duel, Greenburn. The prize is the lady, an' the winner will also be free to hang up his guns, if that's what he wants to do. I dunno about you, Greenburn, but that's what I intend doin'! Yer see, there's been too much cold-blooded killin' in this state. It's time fer it to stop. This is the last chance saloon fer one of us. What d'yer say?'

Floyd's mouth ran dry. This was not the situation he wanted. He knew all about Ervine Fulbeck's reputation as a gunfighter. Most men would want to avoid getting into a duel with him. But he knew he had no choice. He had to take a chance.

'OK,' said Floyd. 'If that's what yer want!' Ervine signalled to his thug 'Sly grin' to guard Sarah.

'D'yer wanna back down to the hotel, Greenburn?'

'OK,' Floyd said. He slowly backed down the street. A few people including Chancy and Russ had congregated on the sidewalk. Floyd stopped outside the hotel.

★　★　★

'Why is Fulbeck backing further up the street?' Sarah asked. 'What's his game?'

'Dunno,' said 'Sly grin'. He belched as he nursed the hangover which meant he had missed the morning's ride to Denton to bring this beautiful woman back to town. 'It'll be a fair fight, though. Duels are always the fairest fights,' he lied. Sarah put her hand over her nose and mouth to avoid breathing in the smell of stale tobacco and alcohol. She felt she had to do something quickly to escape from the clutches of this foul-smelling, leery man and stop the duel from taking place. 'Sly grin' sensed her agitation. He couldn't afford to screw up with the boss twice in one day. He put his arm around Sarah's waist and held her tightly, to prevent her from going anywhere.

* * *

Fulbeck stopped backing up the street. He had reckoned there probably wasn't much to choose between him and Greenburn in terms of speed of draw. Tactically, this gun-fight was going to be won by the more accurate shooter, not the fastest. Distance between the two fighters therefore mattered. The further apart they were, the more chance Fulbeck's customized twelve-inch barrel revolver would have of hitting its target than the five-and-a-half inch one on Greenburn's Peacemaker.

'When you're ready?' Fulbeck shouted out, 'I'll count us in. After the count of three, we draw and fire at will, OK?'

'He's played me for a sucker,' Floyd muttered to himself. He had thought that Fulbeck was going to fire from outside the jail. Instead, not only had the gunfighter increased the distance between them, but he had also managed to take the end of the street with the sun, which was now emerging behind him! If Fulbeck's goin' for accuracy, I'm goin' to have to try an' go for speed, Floyd thought to himself.

A feeling of fear started to course

through his body. It was that same feeling of fear he had felt back in '61, when he was confronted as a young man by a soldier intent on running him through with a bayonet. Floyd felt a dryness in his throat. He glanced over at the frightened Sarah who was being physically restrained by one of Fulbeck's thugs. Floyd pulled the brim of his hat down, ostensibly to shield his eyes from the sun.

'I'm ready!' he shouted out, muttering 'you cowardly bastard,' afterwards under his breath. After the count of three, he drew, getting three shots off in quick succession. Through the gun smoke and the glare of the sun he could make out some movement down the other end of the street, but couldn't see whether he had hit his target or not.

★   ★   ★

The three bullets kicked up dust around Ervine Fulbeck's feet, but he stood firm, legs astride, his left forearm bent across his body at chin height, his right wrist resting on his left forearm, and his head cocked slightly to one side as he aligned the sights of the gun in his right hand. He pulled the trigger and watched as Floyd Greenburn started to sway and lurch. It's all over, he thought. He looked across at his special prize, Sarah Tamswaite. A feeling of euphoria came over him as he realized that he was at last free from the burden he had carried for the last twenty odd years. He lowered his right arm.

⋆ ⋆ ⋆

Still unsteady on his feet, Floyd felt the searing heat on his forehead from the bullet that had pierced his hat. Briefly wondering if it was all over for him, he started to stagger forwards, and managed to fire what he thought would be his last ever shot. The low bullet hit the off-guard Fulbeck in the knee, causing the gunslinger to fall to the ground. Floyd recovered his balance. His next bullet hit Ervine's gun hand, sending the weapon spinning across the street. He walked down the street towards the defeated Fulbeck. Ervine looked up in disbelief. They both knew that Floyd had one bullet left.

'I shot you right through the middle of the forehead!' Fulbeck said in his state of shock.

'I thought you might try to do that,' Floyd said, taking off his hat. 'That's why I concealed my deputy's badge inside the centre of my hat band. I had it made up especially, when I lost the tin one. The new one's made from bronze, and nickel backed, and is designed to stop a bullet. My intuition told me that sooner or later, I was gonna come up against the assassin who shoots his victims through the head.

'My tin star, by the way, turned up on the dead body of Marietta. Remember her? She was shot through the middle of the forehead. And Adison Marson, the curator of the civil war museum, was also shot through the forehead. He was gettin' too close to findin' out Peters' real identity. Oh, and apparently a similar fate befell the two men you rode with in the Civil War. Bullets through the forehead. Those men knew that you couldn't have seen the atrocity from afar, as you claimed in court, Captain Emmett Aldstone, so Peters had you silence 'em! Cos that's your real name, ain't it? You changed your name to Fulbeck to avoid having to answer embarrassing questions, like your co-conspirator, Travis, changed his to Peters.'

'How d'yer work that out, yer son of a bitch?' Aldstone spat the words from his mouth. 'What makes yer so sure you're right?'

'Well, after I first suddenly realized what your true identity might be, it took a while to figure out if all the pieces fitted. But fit they did.' Floyd paused, savouring the moment. 'Wherever there was one of these signature killings, there was always a plausible

270

reason for you, Emmett Aldstone, to be there to shut someone up. I reckoned that it all started when you lied in that courtroom about seein' the massacre, for a share of the Travis fortune. When you accepted that payment, Ransom Travis had you in the palm of his hand. You signed your soul away to the devil that day, an' all the time that Travis was alive, there was no way back. And with him gone, you thought you might have a chance of redemption.

'But there still ain't no way back cos you allowed yerself to get in too deep. It started with killin' anyone who got too close to what really happened that dreadful day in '61, and as time went on, more besides, like Adison and Marietta. You were Travis's lapdog who took care of his dirty work, an' I was gonna be your next victim. Killed in a duel maybe, but shot in exactly the same way as the others, an' fer the same reason.'

'Yer can't prove any of that!' Aldstone said angrily.

'I don't need to,' Floyd retorted. 'Too many coincidences for any jury aroun' here to think you innocent, eh Aldstone?'

'Dammit, Greenburn. Why don't yer kill me now? If you hadn't cheated on me just now, I would have shot you dead, but I would have shown you mercy, like I did the others. A bullet through the head is such a quick way to die, it's painless. So you do the same for me now and shoot me through the head. You've got one bullet left. Put me out of mer misery. Can yer do that?'

'No, Aldstone, cos like you said, the killin's got to stop. My men are here an' they're gonna take yer to Faux-Port to stand trial.'

'If I'm gonna stand trial, it has to be here in Russen. It's the county seat of which I am still the mayor.'

'I don't think it's gonna be fer much longer,' Floyd replied. 'I rode through Faux-Port to get here. Conway MacPherson was there. Many of the miners changed their minds and voted for Faux-Port, as did the people of Denton. Result hasn't been confirmed yet, but it sounds like Russen ain't in it no more.'

★ ★ ★

As Russ and Chancy took Aldstone away, Floyd and Sarah walked slowly down the middle of Main Street, arm in arm.

'Do you think that if Travis and Aldstone hadn't fought in the Civil War, they would have turned out better people?' she asked Floyd.

'It's certainly possible,' Floyd replied. 'War can turn a man's head the wrong way. Make a man do things he never believed he had in him.'

'So why do we have to have war, Floyd?'

'I dunno, but throughout history, men have always fought wars against each other, an' I guess they always will.'

'But this particular war's all over now, isn't it?' Sarah asked.

'Yes, my dear, it is,' Floyd replied.

'The Holmbury County Seat War is finally over.'